EVERYONE A STRANGER

VICTOR WATSON

Catnip

CATNIP BOOKS
Published by Catnip Publishing Ltd
Quality Court, off Chancery Lane
London WC2A 1HR
This edition first published 2013
1 3 5 7 9 10 8 6 4 2
Text copyright © Victor Watson, 2013
The moral rights of the author and illustrator have been asserted.
A CIP catalogue record for this book is available from the British
Library.
ISBN 978-1-84647-161-2
Printed in Poland
www.catnippublishing.co.uk

A long winding street leads from the centre of Great Deeping to the railway line. There are doorways and corners where someone can hide.

Not in daylight, of course. But after nightfall there are deep recesses, each with its extra shadowed double-darkness. Especially during a blackout.

A stranger standing quietly in one of these places could stretch out his arm to passersby. He could touch them. He would be so close that he would smell their tobacco smoke, or perfume. And he'd hear small scraps of private talk. *She'd be taking a risk! Have you got the key? Oh, it's in my bag! You'd think after the last time . . .*

In the winter of 1945 Molly Barnes and Abigail Murfitt – best friends – hurried that way every evening. Carelessly, trustingly.

There had been rumours about someone lurking in the hiding places. But the rumours were as elusive as the lurker. They came and went.

It's still there today, that street.

When Molly thought about Abigail, the word that came

to mind was *faithful*. She never put you down; she never wrapped herself in impenetrable moods; she never sulked; and she never froze you out with chilly silences.

But that year Abigail headed off in some unpredictable directions where Molly found it hard to follow. It started on a cold Friday afternoon in January.

They were on their way home from the school bus. It was almost dark. In their blue school uniforms and with satchels over their shoulders, they felt weightless and happy. They had no homework to do that night. So there would be tea at Abigail's house, then back to Molly's to spend the rest of the evening together.

That's what they always did on Fridays.

There was a handcart in the street, with *GAS BOARD* painted on its side. A ladder was propped against a streetlight and an old man stood on the ladder, cleaning the glass of the lamp.

'Mr Wayne! How can you see what you're doing?' Abigail knew him. He went to her chapel.

He came slowly down the ladder and turned to the girls. 'I've done now, anyway,' he said. 'I'm getting them all ready. As soon as the War's over they can all be turned on again.'

Molly could remember when the street-lights had all been turned off. There was one outside her bedroom. She could remember herself – much younger, in pyjamas, on tiptoe at her window – staring at the softly-lit glass lantern, so close that she could almost touch it.

That was in 1939. But now the War was almost over

and the blackout would end soon. Already, some people were careless about it – a bright window left with the blinds undrawn; a door left open, streaming light across the garden. The air raid wardens would have been onto them like a shot, once. But now no one minded.

The bombing raids had stopped. There hadn't been a German plane over Great Deeping for months. There were the flying-bombs, of course. Buzzbombs, people called them. But lights would make no difference to *them* – they were pilotless, and they exploded wherever they happened to fall. Besides, it was London that was getting the worst of them. And the southern counties.

The War in Europe was coming to an end. The allied armies were closing in on Berlin. Soon, Hitler would be captured, or killed, and Germany would surrender.

Then Molly's dad would come home. He was in Italy, where the War was already over. Everyone else would come home too.

Well, no, *not* everyone. Abigail's father was *missing, feared killed*. Her mum had heard no more about him since the day she'd received that telegram. He was not expected.

When they arrived at Abigail's house, there was the usual smell of cooking. But in the living room they found Mrs Murfitt seated at the table with her head on her folded arms. She looked smaller than usual; crumpled.

'*Mum!* Aren't you feeling well?'

'Sit down, Abigail. I've something to tell you.' Mrs Murfitt was not a person who wasted words.

Abigail gripped Molly's arm. 'Dad?' she whispered. For five years they had lived with the knowledge that they might hear about him at any time.

But Mrs Murfitt shook her head. 'No, it's not about your father.'

'I'd better go,' Molly said. She could see this was a family matter.

But they ignored her. So she stayed.

'It *really* isn't about Dad?' Abigail said quietly.

Mrs Murfitt shook her head. 'It's about your Auntie Sheila.'

Abigail frowned. For years Auntie Sheila had been just a name on Christmas cards and birthday cards. What had faraway Auntie Sheila got to do with them now?

Mrs Murfitt took a deep breath. 'It was a V-1, one of those buzzbombs. It landed on their street. Everyone was killed – except your cousin Ivy. She was at work.'

There was nothing that could be said to news like this, no words for this kind of blank shock.

Abigail slid into a chair beside her mother at the table.

'The thing is, Abigail – Ivy's coming to live with us. Next week.'

'What? Why has she got to come here?' It seemed so bizarre. Impossible!

'She's homeless – and she has no other family.' Mrs Murfitt spoke in a dead flat tone, defeated and bitter.

'Surely she can go somewhere else?' Abigail whispered.

Molly stared at Abigail in surprise.

Mrs Murfitt looked thoughtfully at her daughter. 'Well, she's coming whether you want her or not. She's only eighteen and she has no other relatives.'

Molly, forgetting it was none of her business, asked a question. 'But does she *have* to come? I mean, if she's eighteen?'

'Until she's twenty-one she's a minor. She's underage. What does it *matter*? The point is that she's homeless and we're her only relatives. I am responsible.'

Abigail stared for a moment, then leapt to her feet and made for the kitchen. 'I'm going to start the meal,' she said savagely.

Molly was embarrassed and uncertain what to do. Mrs Murfitt flapped her hand in a way that seemed to mean: *I've* done my best – Molly, *you* try!

So Molly followed Abigail into the kitchen. Two saucepans of prepared vegetables stood on the oven-top and Abigail was trying to light a match. But she struck the match so hard against the box that it broke. She threw the pieces angrily on the floor and tried another. Three more matches were struck, broken and thrown away before Molly said, 'For heaven's sake, Abigail, give them to me!'

She lit the gas rings. 'I don't think your mum's got much choice,' she said.

Abigail glared. 'Don't you understand?' she said passionately. 'She's not coming here just to *visit*! She's coming here to *live*. For always. She'll spoil everything!'

'What will she spoil? Is she some kind of monster?'

'*Us!* She'll spoil *us*!'

Molly was bewildered, and showed it in her face.

But Abigail persisted. 'You and me – we've been like this since we were *born*! And you and me and Adam since we were ten!'

To Abigail, this newcomer meant the end of everything. But Molly, only dimly understanding, said, 'Why should she spoil everything? She might be a really nice person.'

'That would be worse!' Abigail snapped. 'If she's horrible, at least we can hate her!'

But she was growing calmer, a little. She pulled open a drawer and began sorting out some cutlery. 'Oh, why did my stupid aunt have to go and get herself bombed!'

She stared at Molly across the kitchen table. 'I don't want her here!' she said quietly. 'And where will she sleep?'

Then Molly began to understand the gravity of this new situation. The railway house had large generous rooms. But there were only two bedrooms.

2

Adam Swales was their friend. He had lived with Molly since the start of the War, when he'd arrived from London as an evacuee.

He drew pictures – *good* pictures. Everybody said so.

But, back in 1942, at the start of his second year at the grammar school, he'd discovered that there were to be no art classes in his timetable. The boys in 2B could choose art, but Adam's class was to have Latin instead.

Adam hadn't hesitated. He asked to see the headmaster and explained the problem. He remembered to say *sir* in all the right places, and he was polite.

'In this school,' Mr Ricks explained, 'boys in the A stream take Latin, boys in the B stream take art. You are now in 2A. So I'm afraid it's impossible.'

'Why, sir?'

This response surprised Mr Ricks. 'Because I see no reason why a special exception should be made for you.'

'But I'm going to be an artist,' Adam explained.

'Half the boys in your year want to be engine drivers,' the head said. 'Does that mean we should offer classes on trains?'

Adam had with him a fat brown envelope. He tipped the contents onto Mr Ricks' desk – fifty or sixty loose pages, all with drawings on them.

Mr Ricks sent Adam back to his class and looked through the drawings. Then he rang for his secretary. 'Send for Mr Fraser, please.'

Mr Fraser was the art master – a rather rugged old man, but still working because of the shortage of teachers.

One by one, Mr Fraser studied Adam's work. Whole drawings, sketches, fragments, done in pencil, pen-and-ink, charcoal, and coloured chalks.

'In the first year he showed promise, but I had no idea . . . No idea at all!'

'He wants to go on doing art. Of course, you know, he's in 2A.'

'He *should* take art,' Mr Fraser said. 'Definitely.'

The next day the headmaster sent for Adam. 'I cannot change the timetable,' he announced. 'So the only way that you can take art would be to move into 2B – which I am sure you wouldn't want to do.'

'Yes I would,' Adam said.

'Then you may,' Mr Ricks announced grandly.

From that time, Adam had studied art with Mr Fraser. One Saturday he took Adam to his home to spend the day in his workshop. There was an old printing press there, and Adam learned about etching and engraving.

He made linocuts in class, but in Mr Fraser's workshop he made a small wood engraving and printed it.

These Saturday visits became frequent.

Mr Fraser's wife was young. She came quietly in and out of the workshop, bringing tea, cakes, and doing some artwork of her own. Adam found it hard to take his eyes off her. All over the place there were paintings of her, and drawings. He couldn't take his eyes off them either.

Mr Fraser lent Adam several books. Adam sometimes kept them for months – but the teacher didn't mind. He always got them back eventually. 'Have you heard of an artist called Picasso?' he asked Adam one day.

Adam shook his head.

'Pablo Picasso,' Mr Fraser said thoughtfully. 'Not very well known to the general public here – not yet, anyway. But people who know about art find his work very exciting.'

He handed Adam three books. 'I picked these up in Paris, before the War. They're books of poems, and a novel, illustrated by Picasso. Why don't you have a look at them?'

3

Abigail was so angry that she was beyond Molly's reach. 'What about dad's office! Why can't we put a bed in there?' she shouted at her mother.

But she knew it was impossible. Her father had a small work room – which Abigail now regarded as hers – but there was no space for a bed in it.

'I'll move in with Molly. *She's* got plenty of spare rooms!' Well, this was true. Molly's mum ran a guesthouse and there were – most of the time these days – lots of empty rooms.

'You'll do no such thing,' Mrs Murfitt said. 'You'll sleep in *your* room with *your* cousin.'

'She's not my cousin! You call her that, but she's *not*!' Abigail was right: Ivy's mum had been Mrs Murfitt's cousin.

'*Second* cousin then,' Mrs Murfitt snapped. 'Or first cousin once removed. It amounts to the same thing.'

Then a new thought had struck Abigail. '*Not in the same bed?*'

But no. That would be too much! So two single beds were borrowed from Molly's guesthouse and set up in Abigail's bedroom.

Darkness was falling when Abigail and Molly got off the school bus on Tuesday. They were to go straight to the station to meet Ivy on the train from London. So, with satchels and hockey sticks, the two girls set off through the town.

'Did you tell Adam?' Abigail asked.

Molly nodded.

'He won't be interested anyway,' Abigail said. 'Unless he wants to draw her.'

Molly sighed. There was some truth in that.

'Abigail?' Molly said halfway along the Station Road. 'What?'

'We heard from my dad. He's coming home on leave.'

Molly had been nervous of sharing this information. Abigail's dad would never be coming on leave and Abigail could be forgiven if she felt bitter when other people's fathers came home safely. But she brightened up immediately. '*Good!*' she said. 'When?'

Abigail has a responsive and generous nature, Molly thought gladly. *(Except where Ivy is concerned.)*

There were just the two of them waiting at the station. One at each end of the platform so that they shouldn't miss Ivy in the dark. Molly was at the end where the engine would stop. Tucking her school mac firmly under her behind, she hoisted herself up onto the top bar of the railings at the back of the platform and lost herself in thought. It started to rain.

15

She was brought sharply out of her thoughts by the clanging of the station bell. Then at Abigail's end of the station old Nobby Clark came down from the signal box and closed the crossing gates against traffic. Half a mile along the track, Abigail's mum would be doing the same with her crossing gates. The way was being cleared for the arrival of Ivy Westgate.

The locomotive heaved and hissed itself to a massive standstill, almost directly opposite Molly. The fireman leaned on the rail of the cab, looking nonchalantly down at her as she jumped from the railings and smoothed her crumpled mac. The stationmaster shouted, '*Deep*ing! *Deep*ing! *Great* Deeping!'

Nine or ten people got out of the train. Workers and shoppers hurried briskly towards the exit. A returning prisoner-of-war limped more slowly, looking around him, taking it all in. His wife stepped anxiously forward, leaving the pram aside.

Ivy hasn't come! Molly thought at first. What a relief that would be! They would have a reprieve. They could spend the evening by themselves, joyous and free. Perhaps Ivy wasn't coming at all, ever.

But Ivy *had* come. Molly could see a figure in the gloom at the other end of the train, closer to where Abigail stood. She had stepped down onto the platform with a suitcase and was now turning back to get another from the compartment.

Abigail greeted her. Politely, but not enthusiastically. Molly ran up and tried to do better.

In the dark, it was impossible to size up the new arrival – except that she wore a thick overcoat, belted tight, and a headscarf. She was no taller than they were, but she looked grown up. ('She needn't think she's going to be boss!' Abigail had said. Now Molly knew what Abigail meant.)

The other passengers were all heading in the same direction. So, naturally, Ivy followed them. 'Not that way,' Molly said. 'There's a short-cut.'

Abigail and Molly picked up Ivy's two suitcases. (*Heavy!* Abigail thought angrily. *Is this all she possesses in the world?* Molly wondered.) Ivy took the two hockey sticks, but when she offered to carry Abigail's satchel as well, Abigail twitched her shoulder sharply away. (*Giving her the cold shoulder*, Molly thought.)

Along the platform they led the newcomer, down the slope at the end, and on to the path that led – unofficially – alongside the level crossing. Beside them, the back-end of the train slid quietly away; all the noise was at the front.

Nobby Clark had already come down his steps to open the gates. 'This your new evacuee then?' he shouted. All the railway staff knew Abigail.

Abigail grunted something.

'Left it a bit late, een't she?' Nobby said. 'The War's over, nairly!'

Then along the cinder path through the goods yard, by the gasworks, and so to the grassy track that ran beside the railway.

'How she *talked*!' Molly told her mum later. 'Non-stop! She just went on and on.'

It was Molly who had started it. All three of them seemed tongue-tied at first. Molly couldn't think of anything to say and Abigail maintained a resolute silence. Eventually Molly asked Ivy if she'd had a good journey. It was a meaningless thing to say – but it was enough to set Ivy going.

'Oh, yes! It was all right at first. There were all these servicemen in the same compartment as me! There were two soldiers and three airmen. No, I tell a lie! It was *three* soldiers and *two* airmen. One of them was ever so good-looking. He gave me a cigarette. I don't smoke, not really, but I couldn't refuse.

'– They were ever such fun. Laugh? The things they said! One of them said I had nice legs. Cheeky blighter!

'– Well, I *have*, actually.

' – One of them said I was no better than I ought to be. *Cheek!* I said. I asked him if *he* was better than he ought to be. They didn't half laugh!

'– D'you know, whenever the train went round a bend or something, the one sitting next to me leant against me. Pressed his shoulder against mine, ever so hard. I told him, I said, *Lay off doing that! You'll have me out of the train!* He did look a fool. But they all got out at Cambridge.

'– It was *awful* after that. This man got in. He was a prisoner-of-war coming home. He told me he was in some prison camp in Germany and the Yanks

18

captured it and let all the prisoners out.

'– You'd think he'd be a bit more cheerful! But he was a miserable old so-and-so. Trouble was, he had only half a face! Well, one ear was missing, and some of his hair.

'– And he sat right opposite me. I didn't know where to look!

'– It ain't half *dark*! Is this it, then? Are we there? Oh, Lor!'

Heedless of the blackout, Mrs Murfitt stood at the open back door with the light streaming out into the garden. There were greetings and taking off of coats, putting down of suitcases – enough more-or-less to conceal the fact that Abigail was still silent.

Molly was to stay for tea. Abigail had insisted.

Adam would come later to walk Molly back home. There had been talk about a man who'd been lurking in the streets. One of the Italian POWs, people said. They called them Eye-ties. But it couldn't be one of them, because they were always back in their camp by five. And the Lurker never started his prowling until after dark.

He wasn't seen often. Two or three weeks would pass by with no sight of him. Then one evening, after dark, someone would see him again – or *think* so.

Molly wasn't scared of Lurkers. But she liked Adam coming to take her home.

Ivy chatted all through the meal, telling them about her work in the munitions factory. 'I only tightened nuts,' she said. 'They didn't think I was clever enough for anything else! Boy, was I glad to see the back of that spanner!'

After tea, she helped with the washing-up. 'Why does your mum keep going outside?' she whispered loudly to Abigail. 'Has she got the runs or something?'

This more or less forced Abigail to speak. 'She has to open and close the crossing gates whenever there's a train,' she explained grudgingly.

Ivy pulled a *fancy that!* face. 'Oh!' she said.

Later, Adam arrived. With him was Molly's little brother, William, aged five, holding Adam's hand and gravely studying Ivy. Adam said hullo and asked Ivy about where she'd lived in London, what kind of bomb it had been.

Then he lost interest. *He won't be drawing her then,* Molly thought.

It was almost eight o'clock when they left. Neither of them believed in the Lurker, but in the darkness of the street young William held tightly onto both their hands.

4

Molly's younger brother William never spoke. He had never uttered a single word in his life. No *ma-ma* or *da-da*, nothing at all. He had learned to stand up on his own, to crawl, to walk – all more or less when a growing baby should. Later, he had learned to feed himself, not to need nappies, to dress himself – all when you would expect him to.

He would laugh, cry, scream when tickled. And he would hum a nursery tune and get it right. He would nod or shake his head. But he never said anything.

Yet, somehow, he always managed to make himself understood. Molly would feel a gentle tug on her skirt, or a touch on her arm – and there would be William, pointing at something. When he started school, his teacher told them how clever he was at getting the other children to help him. He didn't miss out on anything.

Mrs Barnes was worried about it. She had written to her husband in Italy and he suggested William should be taken to see a doctor. *But we can't afford a doctor*, Mrs Barnes thought. She would find money to pay the doctor for measles, or pneumonia, or an injury, but should you spend money because your little boy never said anything?

In spite of the expense, she took William to see Dr Pearson, who said she was quite right to have come and would she like him to arrange for the little boy to be seen by a specialist in Cambridge?

More money, of course. But it was settled: William was to go to Addenbrookes Hospital for a thirty-minute consultation.

The consultant, Mr Anstruther, was old, but conscientious and kindly. He spent much more than the paid-for thirty minutes on them. Young William was given a physical examination to check his breathing, his hearing, his vocal chords, and his palate and tongue. He was given instructions, which he obeyed with perfect understanding. He was given intelligence tests which he thought were games.

'I'll be writing to your doctor,' Mr Anstruther said. 'But I can tell you now – there is absolutely nothing wrong with William. Nothing at all. He isn't deaf and he isn't dumb. He is what we call an *elective mute*.'

Molly knew *mute*. She worked out *elective* in her head.

'An *elective mute* is a person, usually a child, who *chooses* not to talk. Really that is all you need to know. William would rather not talk. That's his choice.'

'But what should we do?'

'There's nothing you can do. Just wait for him to change his mind.'

Mr Anstruther gave Molly's mum a small book called *Mutism and How to Help*. So they left, holding young William's hands and not quite sure whether they should feel disheartened or cheered.

As they were leaving Mr Anstruther said, 'When William does decide to say something, it'll probably come out as a perfect sentence. Perfectly phrased and perfectly expressed!'

5

In south London there was a place called Mercer's Lane Market. The people there that January morning were pale and pinched with cold. With poverty, too, and sleepless nights. Tiny white pellets of frozen snow stung their faces like handfuls of grit. Miniature snowdrifts a quarter of an inch deep built up against the objects on sale.

Into the market, with his collar up against the cold, walked Bob Swales, Adam's dad, newly promoted to Divisional Officer in the National Fire Service. He was much liked, and several people greeted him.

There were lots of stalls: makeshift trestle tables; wheeled carts; one or two hand-barrows. But they didn't have much to sell – secondhand (or thirdhand) clothes; boots and shoes; ancient crockery (none of it matching); cutlery. And vegetables grown on local allotments, or brought in from Kent. Leeks, potatoes, carrots, parsnips, that sort of thing.

The dealers didn't look as if they expected to sell much. And the buyers had hardly any money. Most of them were women, children and old men. There *was* one young man, Dickie Benbow, an army corporal home on leave, wearing his khaki uniform and helping his mum with her stall. *It's good to hear his voice in the market again*, people said. *Shout? You should hear him! They should've made him a drill instructor.*

Tramlines ran along the street, but they were rusty and disused. A V-1 buzzbomb had blown up a section of the track a few streets away. That was in November. *Lord knows when they'll get round to repairing the line*, people said.

The buzzbomb had fallen in Bob's area and he'd organised the rescue operation. It was a miserable business. Those V-1s carried a ton of high explosives in their warheads. A *ton*! It blasted the railway viaduct, shattering everything for around a hundred yards and pouring huge chunks of brickwork on to the houses below.

Some people never heard the blast. Others were buried alive by the falling masonry. People were dragged from the rubble, covered in dust, their clothes torn, their eyes confused, and their hair in stiff spikes. But Bob Swales had never lost his cool. He'd kept everyone calm and got everything done.

One of the stallholders called out. 'Swalesy! You OK?'

'Yes, mate. I had a good night's sleep last night. For once!'

'Me too! Hitler must be losin' his touch.'

Everyone in the market was hard up. You could tell by their clothes. But there was one well-dressed man.

Just one – wearing a trilby hat and a smart overcoat with a fur collar to keep his throat warm. None of the people in the market knew his name. But they all knew his type.

Two military policemen came strolling along the street, in step with one another, with a watchful look in their eyes. They didn't half fancy themselves, those red-caps! The man in the overcoat changed at once. No one saw him move – yet in an instant he had a slight stoop, and he looked older. Amazing it was. But young Dickie just checked that his tunic was properly done up – then he carried on weighing out a pound of Spanish onions. (*Spanish? You must be joking! They were grown beside a railway line in Hackney.*)

The military policemen turned into a side street, and the man with the fur collar breathed easy again.

He was joined by another man, older, also smartly dressed, but less showy, and smaller in build. People who knew him called him the Maggot.

They didn't greet each other. The smaller man just said quietly, 'What you got?'

'Twenty RAF greatcoats, two pound each.'

'What colour?'

'What d'you mean, *what colour*? RAF blue, what d'you *think*!'

'Well, they're no use to me! Unless you can get 'em dyed. Get 'em dyed black and I'll give you *one* pound each. What else?'

'Fifty ARP tin helmets.'

'Don't waste my time, Frosty! Everyone's got tin hats! I can't sell them.'

Frosty sighed. 'A box of adjustable spanners. Brand new.' Then, in a lower voice, 'War Department.'

'How many?'

'About eighty.'

'That's more like it. But I'll take a look before I pay you for 'em. What else?'

'Not much. Some beads.'

'*Beads?*'

'Strings of glass beads. For necklaces. A shilling each.'

'Where are they?'

Frosty pulled a package from inside his overcoat and passed it to the Maggot.

Bob Swales was chatting to an old lady crouching over two walking sticks. 'How's that boy of yours?' she asked him. She was so bent she could hardly raise her face to look at him.

'He's OK.'

'Still drawin' pictures?'

Bob Swales laughed. 'Yes. He's still drawin' his pictures.'

'They'll be comin' home soon. All those kids.'

'Hope so,' Bob said.

While the beads were being examined, Frosty said, 'I've not seen Willy Wilson lately. He's all right, I suppose?'

The Maggot didn't move a muscle. 'Willy won't be around for a while,' he said.

'Why not? Is he ill?'

'You could say that, Frosty. You could definitely say that. He annoyed me – and then he got ill. Understand?'

'What d'you mean?'

'He annoyed me *a lot*. So he's *very* ill, know what I mean? I'll give you a penny each for these. They're rubbish, but I might be able to get rid of 'em for tuppence apiece.'

6

Mrs Barnes decided they should keep a few hens, for the eggs. So one weekend they'd built a chicken run in the backyard, with nesting boxes and a walk-in door. Adam finished off the work by painting a fiery red cockerel over the chicken run door.

But when Molly's dad came home on leave, the sight of these changes to his backyard – and half a dozen hens scratching freely in the garden – had thrown him into a fury. He'd raged about decisions taken in his absence, and outsiders coming in and changing his home beyond recognition.

The *outsider* was Adam. But Molly's mum had come to their defence and explained that it was her idea – and where did he think those eggs had come from that he'd enjoyed the previous night when he arrived on the midnight train?

The row had blown over. But they all knew (though nobody said) that Mr Barnes disliked having Adam in his house.

Molly pestered her dad to tell stories about what he'd

done in North Africa, what had happened to him in Italy, and what it was like to cross the Mediterranean in a troop ship.

He tried to oblige her, but his heart wasn't in it. 'When we're sitting around in camp,' he said, 'it's the *future* we talk about – we make plans for when the War's over. All the time.'

They were all there – his wife, Molly, Abigail, and Adam. Ivy too, shy and silent. Young William sat on the floor, herding glass marbles across the carpet with a ruler.

'We think about nothing else,' he said. '*When will we get demobbed? Will someone be at the station to meet us? What will we have for our first civvy meal?* You'd be the same, Molly. We don't want to talk about the past. We're looking *ahead*!'

He was different this time, Molly thought. Before, when he'd come home on leave, he'd worn his civilian clothes, but they'd looked uncomfortable and temporary. *This* time, however, he wore his civvies in readiness for the real thing. And he was full of fiery energy. Had he been like that before the War? She couldn't remember. She'd been too young.

'When do you think the War will be over?' she asked him. He was a soldier; he ought to know, she thought.

But he said what everyone said. 'A few months perhaps. It can't be long! The allied armies are closing in on Berlin. Hitler's done for!'

'Back to normal,' Molly said.

30

But then he startled her. '*No!*' he said sharply, almost angrily. 'There must be no going back to that old world! No more wars. No more poverty. *This* time we must get it right.'

'Normal for us,' Abigail said, '*is* the War.'

It was true, Molly thought. She had only hazy memories of what it had been like before it all started, in 1939.

'And no more spivs getting rich while the rest of us do the fighting and the working!'

Abigail smiled. Her mum was always going on about spivs.

'First we have to get rid of Churchill,' Molly's dad said.

Molly couldn't believe her ears. Mr Churchill was her hero, the man who'd got them through the War, the man who'd kept their hearts up – even in those dark days in 1940 when the Germans were expected to invade.

'All that's true, Molly. But he's a man of war. We need a different kind of leader for peacetime.'

'That's what my mum says too,' Abigail said.

'As soon as the War's over there'll be a general election – and that'll be the last of Churchill. You'll see!'

One by one, Molly's certainties were collapsing. She felt almost tearful at the injustice of it. 'But surely the country won't vote for *Mr Attlee*?' she said. She was disbelieving and indignant. *That* funny little man!

Ivy stared. Abigail suspected she didn't know who

Mr Attlee was. She had a habit when she didn't understand something of twisting down her lower lip; not exactly a sneer, but as if to say why should *she* care?

'Well, I'll tell you this,' Mr Barnes said. 'The forces won't vote for Churchill. *They'll* have a vote too, remember – wherever they are in the world. As far away as Burma and the Far East – everyone will vote. And they all want a Labour government, not Winston Churchill.'

'What makes you so sure?' his wife asked.

'Because they believe that Mr Attlee will get them demobbed faster. If Churchill wins, he'll keep us all in the army for years!'

Mr Barnes helped himself to some more sausages from the pan. Back at the table, he warmed to his theme.

'I've big plans for what we're going to do with this place,' he said. 'My *Post-War Plan for the Future.*'

Then he told them what he'd spent his time thinking about. 'There's no hotel in Great Deeping now, not since the Crown was bombed. We're going to upgrade! The Ely Guesthouse will become a proper hotel – *the* hotel in the town.'

Molly liked that idea. 'But,' she said, 'please can we change its name?' She had always thought the Ely Guesthouse was a silly thing to call a guesthouse in Great Deeping. Ely was ten miles away!

'Yes, we can,' her dad said eagerly. 'What shall we call it?'

'The Great Deeping Hotel,' Molly suggested.

Abigail made her small contribution to changing history. 'The *Deeping Hotel* sounds neater,' she said.

The others agreed. It did. So the *Deeping Hotel* it was to be.

Then Mr Barnes announced that he'd already arranged for decorators to repaint the bedrooms – all of them – starting in a couple of weeks.

Molly felt she couldn't keep up with this. It made her excited and jumpy, but apprehensive.

'There's another thing,' Mr Barnes said. 'There's a special government plan for small businessmen.'

'Are you a small businessman?'

'Definitely. They'll try to post people like me to places near their homes. So we can get home at weekends and get things started.'

It was impossible not to get caught up in Mr Barnes' excitement.

'Gradually things will get back to normal. Evacuees will go home . . . '

Out of the corner of her eye, Molly saw Adam's drawing hand freeze for perhaps three seconds. Then it carried on as if nothing had happened.

'*When* will they?' she said.

'Pretty fast, I can tell you that!' her dad said. 'Once peace comes, you don't think anyone's going to pay for evacuees, do you?'

It seemed to Molly that the whole conversation had been a trick, and those words had been slipped in as if they were of no importance. *Evacuees will go home.*

'Time for you two to take Abigail and Ivy home,' Mrs Barnes said later.

Mr Barnes looked puzzled. 'Can't they go back on their own?' His tone of voice meant: *What are you fussing for? There aren't any air raids now!*

'There's been someone hanging about around this end of the town,' Mrs Barnes said. 'After dark. I'd rather Adam went with them.'

'It's our Lurker,' Abigail said cheerfully. She didn't believe in him; nor did Molly.

7

One Saturday, when Adam was at Mr Fraser's house, a
guest arrived – a Mr Paterson Royce. Mrs Fraser
introduced him to Adam and the four of them sat
together in the artists' workshop. Adam was making a
pen-and-ink copy of an old engraving and Mr Fraser's
young wife was working on an oil painting.

Mr Paterson Royce was an art dealer. So it was not
surprising that he asked to look through Adam's current
sketchbook. 'They're quite good,' he remarked. 'But the
line is immature.'

'It would be surprising if his line were *not* immature,'
Mr Fraser replied. 'Adam is fifteen.'

Mr Royce had strong views. 'The trouble with boys
like you is that you simply don't know who you are!'
Mr Royce said.

Adam looked up, mildly bemused.

'It's called an identity crisis. It's common in boys of
your age. Especially in boys of your class.'

'My class?' Adam wasn't sure if he was talking about
school.

'Yes. I've seen it before. As I said, you've not found
out who you are.'

Mr Royce left soon afterwards and Mr Fraser went with him to the front door. Adam and the art teacher's young wife were left together in the studio. Adam was very conscious of her. He always was. All the time, she'd been working quietly, straight-backed at her easel.

She said in her low voice, '*Do* you have an identity crisis, Adam?'

Adam knew he should be polite about the Frasers' guest, but he couldn't help himself. 'He's barmy! How can anyone *not* know who they are?'

He saw the side of her cheek change shape a little as she smiled. 'He came down especially to see your work. My husband told him about you. He's very impressed.'

Adam absorbed this. 'He might like my drawings, but he's wrong about me,' he said. '*I* know who I am, whatever *he* thinks!'

'Yes,' she said softly. 'I believe you do.'

She turned to face him then and they shared a smile, mischievous and conspiratorial. Two people who knew exactly who they were.

Molly followed Adam into his bedroom one afternoon and knelt on his bed, facing him, wanting to chat.

'Ivy's got herself a job,' she said. 'At the shirt factory in Littleport. She says she's used to factories.'

Molly had noticed there were times when Ivy seemed lost in thought. Lost in *vacancy*, she suspected. Once, when Ivy was washing up at the kitchen sink, she'd stopped and stared out of the window, leaning motionless with her hands in the water. For minutes on end.

Molly had risked showing sympathy. 'Thinking about your mum?' she asked.

But Ivy just said, 'What, *her*?' and pulled a face.

Telling this to Adam, Molly asked him why he hadn't wanted to draw Ivy. 'There's not much there to draw,' he said.

Artists can be very cruel, Molly thought. (She also thought, *he draws* me *all the time.*)

'Abigail hates sharing her bedroom,' she said.

Adam was studying the foreshortening of Molly's knees and thighs as she knelt, facing him. 'I don't see why she should,' he said. 'When you're in your bedroom, you're asleep most of the time. So why should it matter who's with you?'

That was pretty rich, coming from Adam, Molly thought. 'Have you forgotten those nightmares you used to have?' she said.

About three years ago, Adam had been troubled by what he called blitz-mares. Night after night he would awaken, frightened and shaking. This had gone on for weeks. Almost every night he would bring his eiderdown (illicitly) into Molly's room, where he would sleep in peace, and without dreams.

When Molly's mum found out, she told Adam to *draw* his nightmares. Draw them, she said, then *burn* them.

That had worked and the nightmares had stopped. Molly had been disappointed. 'It mattered then who was with you in the bedroom,' she reminded him.

'Do you *want* to go back to London?' She hadn't planned to ask him that. It just came out.

'It won't happen yet,' Adam said. 'Not while the V-1s and V-2s keep coming.'

'But after that?'

He pulled a comically sad face, like a circus clown's. 'No. I want to stay here – at least until the end of next year, when we take our School Cert.'

I shall have to be content with that, Molly thought.

'I've written to my dad,' Adam said.

'Written?' Adam usually sent pictures.

He grinned. 'Yes, *written*! A proper letter.'

8

The stallholders in Mercer's Lane market were beginning to pack up for the day. It was cold, and darkness was coming down early.

'About those greatcoats,' Frosty said.

'What greatcoats?'

'The RAF greatcoats! I told you about 'em! You said you'd take them if I got them dyed.'

The Maggot shook his head. 'I got no use for greatcoats,' he said. 'I don't care whether they're khaki or sky-blue-pink, they're still ex-WD greatcoats! Now if you can get me any more of them spanners . . . '

'But I paid good money . . .'

The smaller man took hold of Frosty's fur collar.

'Listen, Frosty. Things are changing, OK? The War's nearly over. Soon there'll be more money about. People will want to buy different kinds of stuff. Understand? *Quality* stuff. Not greatcoats and cheap beads.'

'I dunno what you mean.'

'I mean I'm widening my clee-on-tell. *That's* what I mean – widening my clee-on-tell. And if you and me are goin' to do business together, you'll have to get hold of a different kind of stuff. Widen your range. Know what I'm sayin'?'

There was a third man with them this time, by the name of Jimmy Riddle. That wasn't his real name, of course. *Rider* he was, Jimmy Rider. But he'd always been called Jimmy Riddle.

Divisional Officer Bob Swales and his driver, Firewoman Nancy Turner, were having a break at a Salvation Army tea wagon.

Bob had been reading a letter. As Nancy turned towards him with two mugs of tea, he folded it up and pushed it into a pocket in his tunic.

'Not bad news I hope, sir?' she said. She'd noticed the thoughtful look on his face.

'Well, no,' he said. 'A letter from my son.'

'Adam, isn't it?'

He nodded.

'Well, a letter's good.'

Bob liked Nancy. She had plenty of pluck. She'd given up her job as a librarian to work for the Fire Service. Not much more than a schoolgirl, really.

'That's the trouble,' he said. 'It's a *letter*. He never sends letters. Only pictures. Just enough to show me what's going on.'

'*Pictures?*'

'Yep. It's the same with his mum. She gets pictures too. But this one's a letter.'

He stirred his tea thoughtfully. 'Well, at least I know now he can write sentences. He can spell properly, too.'

Two passing airmen wolf-whistled at Nancy, and walked on. Nancy, hardly bothering to turn her head, told them calmly and obscenely what to do.

'I've got some time-off owed to me,' Bob said. 'I think I'll take a couple of days and go and see him.'

'A break would do you good, sir.'

Frosty was depressed by all this talk of future developments in the Black Market. So he changed the subject. 'How's Willy Wilson?' he said. 'Is he any better?'

'Willy? No, he ain't. They're buryin' him on Friday.'

'You mean . . . ?'

'Three o'clock at All Saints Church. You comin'? I shall have to be there – I've paid for the ruddy flowers. And I want to see I get my money's worth.'

Frosty was really shaken by this news, you could tell. He looked nervously at Jimmy Riddle. 'Did you know he was dead?'

Jimmy nodded dolefully. 'It was me what found him! He was *marked*, mate,' he said softly. 'Neatly marked! And the police ain't got a clue!'

At that moment there was a change of atmosphere. A convoy of open army trucks was crossing the top of the market, on the main road. They were carrying German prisoners-of-war, thirty or so in the back of each truck. On their way to Waterloo Station, probably. There'd been thousands of POWs lately. On the side of one of the trucks someone had painted the words *LOOK OUT HITLER! HERE WE COME!*

Everyone stared. They probably half-expected to see brutal-looking soldiers, with hard square faces and grim metal helmets. But they weren't like that, not this lot. Their uniforms didn't match; some of them didn't have proper uniforms at all; and their faces were dirty, unshaven, pale. They were hungry and cold – scared too, probably.

Except one of them. He was young and good-looking, wearing an Afrika Corps cap and a woollen scarf round his neck. *He* wasn't bothered, not that one! He stared at the people in the market, showing his contempt for everything British.

There must have been a hold-up in the traffic, for the convoy came to a halt. And at that very moment the sirens began to go, all across south London.

Bob and Nancy put down their teas and paid attention. The three men who were discussing the future of the Black Market went quiet.

Almost immediately everyone heard it. The familiar sound of a flying-bomb – a buzzbomb. A little boy started to wail. Some people hurried off to the nearest shelter, others crouched under the market-stalls; some just stood and stared as the sound grew nearer. No one knew what was for the best with these V-1s: if you stayed outside you could be cut to bits by flying glass, but if you went in search of shelter you might be crushed to death by buildings collapsing.

Even the sparrows went quiet.

It was a truly terrifying noise, like a hundred

motorbikes blasting across the sky. But worse than the noise would be the silence. Everyone knew that when the engine cut out there would be a ten-second delay, then the bomb would crash-land and you'd hear the explosion. If it passed over you, you were relieved – but you felt ashamed too because you knew someone else was going to cop it.

This one passed right over the market, above their heads – an ugly cross-shaped plane, with squared-off wings and no pilot, unutterably menacing.

Then the sky went quiet. And that was worse. The sounds of London seemed muffled and far away. And while everyone stared up at the sky, counting out the seconds, the smart young POW gave the Hitler salute and shouted at the top of his voice, *Sieg Heil! Sieg Heil!*

The fellow prisoners in his truck straightened their backs, held up their heads and took up the cry. Together they chanted triumphantly, over and over, *Sieg Heil! Sieg Heil! Sieg Heil!*

It was a scary moment. It seemed an outrage to hear such a thing shouted in a London street. But there was a British soldier in the back of the truck, with a .303 and his bayonet fixed. The bystanders couldn't hear what he said. But, whatever it was, he put a stop to the chanting. And at that moment the traffic started to move again and the prisoners-of-war almost fell over as their truck jerked forward. The driver probably did it on purpose.

Bob Swales only managed to count to eight. Then

they felt the explosion, a great thump of noise, followed by a blast of air – outwards first, and then sucked back in. The tray of cutlery on the tea wagon tinkled and shook. Then came sounds of screaming and masonry falling. A massive billow of smoke and dust poured into the sky. Two streets away.

World War II was not over yet.

'Come on!' Bob Swales muttered. 'Leave the car – it'll be quicker on foot.'

As he and Nancy raced out of the market in the direction of the explosion, already you could hear the bells of the ambulances and fire engines racing to the incident.

'That was a near thing,' the Maggot muttered.

But Frosty – in spite of his thick overcoat and fur collar – just shivered and felt sick.

9

Before Mr Barnes' leave had ended, he'd asked Deeping's two main painters and decorators, the Pettit brothers, to begin redecorating almost the entire guesthouse, inside and out. And a new sign was to be painted, saying *The Deeping Hotel*.

So there was to be an upheaval. There were lots of rooms, most of them unoccupied, and they were all going to have to be cleared for redecorating, turn and turn about.

There was only one paying guest, a travelling salesman called Mr Elmore Whymper. He was a regular visitor there, a flabby, rather shy man who collected seaside postcards. So quiet that you could be in the same room with him for hours and forget he was there. All his possessions were contained in two suitcases, one of which (securely locked) held his entire collection of postcards.

So it was easy to move Mr Whymper into a different room. Molly's room was slightly more difficult – she was untidy by nature. William was untidy too – but since neither of them had many possessions, moving into different rooms was straightforward.

But Adam's room was a different matter.

A whole day was set aside for all these moves and everyone was going to help. Ivy joined in too, because it was a Saturday and she had nothing else to do. It became something of a festive day – especially since Adam's dad was expected to arrive that evening and stay until Monday.

'Oh my Lor!' Ivy said when she first went into Adam's room. 'We'll have to throw out most of this lot.' Adam stared at her coldly.

It was obvious that Ivy had never seen a room like Adam's. There was paper everywhere – under the bed, on the bed, around the bed; on shelves and chairs and the chest of drawers; on the windowsill; stuck to the walls with brown sticky paper. ('There's to be no more of *that* when the room's been repainted!'). There were pencils everywhere too – crayons, pastels, chalks and a cigar box full of bits of charcoal.

'Do you like your new room, Adam?' Mrs Barnes asked.

He did, quite.

'*Good!* Because I'm not sure I can face moving all this stuff back again.'

Ivy was more excited than they'd ever seen her. She spent more time looking at Adam's drawings than moving his stuff.

'Crikey!' she exclaimed. She'd opened a sketchbook and found Molly looking out at her. Ivy looked from the portrait to Molly and back again. There were

46

drawings of Abigail, too, and William.

'You could see,' Molly said later, 'that she was beginning to understand.' Abigail thought she'd just looked stupefied.

Abigail and Molly – carrying bundles of papers into the new bedroom and coming back for more – would find Ivy still there, gazing at yet another of Adam's drawings. She was transfixed.

She picked up a fat brown folder. It had the word *Picasso* written on the front. 'What's *Picasso*?' she said.

'It's a Spanish food,' Adam explained. 'A sort of sausage. A *spicy* sausage.'

But Molly told her she was having her leg pulled. 'He's a Spanish artist,' she said.

'*You!*' Ivy exclaimed and thumped Adam on the chest.

She opened the folder. Inside was a book, in French, and several sheets of immaculate paper, stiff and white, each with a perfect pen-and-ink drawing on it.

'Yeuch!' Ivy exclaimed. 'I'm glad I don't look like *her!*'

She flipped through the others. 'Some of these are *rude*! And this Picasso of yours must have known some weird-looking women. This one's got two faces!'

'But they're nice faces,' Adam said innocently. 'If *you* had such a nice face, wouldn't you like to have two of them?' He was in a teasing mood.

It dawned on Ivy that the drawings were copies of the illustrations in the book. 'Are you allowed to do that?' she said. 'Can't you draw your own pictures?'

'Artists often make copies to practise,' Abigail said.

Ivy pulled one of her *fancy that* faces and closed the folder. 'Well, I'm off!' she said. 'It's getting on for five and we're going to the Rex at Ely.'

'Who's *we*?' Abigail wanted to know.

'Me and someone else,' Ivy said tartly.

She often did that. For two or three days she would join in with the others as if she'd lived with them all her life; and then she'd go off and do something on her own. Abigail said it was to remind them that she counted as a grown-up and could do what she pleased.

When Adam's room was almost cleared, there was a ring on the front door-bell. Mrs Barnes called up to them. 'Adam, it's your dad!'

They liked Mr Swales. Abigail, fascinated by his stories of the blitz, asked him to explain about V-1s and V-2s. 'I know what V-1s are,' she said. 'But I don't understand about V-2s.'

They were all having supper in Mrs Barnes' kitchen (except Mr Whymper, who was in his room, and Ivy, who'd gone to the pictures). William had been allowed to stay up late and was trying to fence in his herd of marbles by fixing elastic bands round the feet of Molly's chair.

Mr Swales sighed. 'We all thought the War was nearly over. But it isn't! Not for us Londoners anyway! Just when we began to think the War wouldn't last much longer – it's started all over again. With these rockets.'

Molly brought him back to the question Abigail had asked. 'What's the difference between a V-1 and a V-2?' she said.

'The V-1 is exactly what we call it – a *flying bomb*. A bomb with an engine and wings. It flies like a plane, until it cuts out and crashes.'

An elastic band pinged audibly, and William did a little gasp and sat back on his heels, urgently sucking a finger. He held it up to Molly, who kissed it better.

'But a V-2 is a *rocket*. It goes out into space, and then comes down on its target. At a *tremendous* speed. And we can't intercept them.'

'How fast?'

'It hits its target faster than the speed of sound. Around a ton of explosives.'

They took this in, the speed of it, the vast and ruinous scale of it. And the fact that there was no defence, and no escape.

'Why are they called V-2s?'

'The V is for some German word. It means *Vengeance*. Hitler knows he's done for, and he wants to get his own back on as many people as he can. And it's number 2 because the buzzbombs were V-1s.'

'Is it true,' Adam said, 'that you can't hear them coming?'

Bob Swales nodded. 'They fly faster than the speed of sound.'

Molly, Abigail and Adam all did physics at school and they understood the theory that something might travel faster than the speed of sound. But understanding wasn't the same as believing. They couldn't *imagine* what it meant. It seemed like an evil magic.

'If you're in the vicinity when a V-2 lands,' Bob Swales said, 'you get the explosion and then – *afterwards* – you hear the rocket coming. The victims don't hear anything at all, poor buggers. They're dead before the sound reaches them.'

Mrs Barnes wondered if she should protest about *buggers*, but decided not.

'And I'll tell you this,' Bob Swales went on. 'If Adolf Hitler had invented them at the start of the War instead of now, we would all have been wiped out.'

Molly couldn't quite cope with the grimness of this. 'Then we'd all be poor dead buggers,' she said.

'*Molly!*' Mrs Barnes said sharply.

Next morning, Sunday, Adam and his father had their talk.

'Adam, it's out of the question.

'– I'm sorry, son. But once the War's over, no one's going to pay for evacuees to stay in places like this. You'll all be coming home.

'– *London* is your home.

'– I'm proud of you, Adam. Really proud of you and what you're good at. But that doesn't alter the fact that you'll have to come home. A boy's place is with his mum and dad.

'– Yes, I know. But the government will be building thousands of new apartments for everyone who's been bombed out. I've put our name down for one of them.

'– You'll go to a school in London. And they'll have good art teachers there too.

'– All right! We'll *find* a school with a good art teacher.

'– There's no point in going on about this, Adam. Me and your mum, we want a bit of family life, the three of us together.

'– No, I haven't spoken to her yet. But that's what she wants too.

'– You're *so* like your mother. She sometimes gets daft ideas too. I never know where I am with you two!'

Mr Swales left the room then – and Adam saw that Mr Whymper had been there all the time, reading a newspaper unnoticed in an armchair.

'What did your dad say?' Molly asked him afterwards.

Adam shrugged. 'It's no good.' He made his sad-faced-clown look.

Inside Molly's head a voice from when she was about eight years old wailed, *it's not fair!*

But another knowledge told her that complaining about fairness had never changed anything when she was eight. And it wasn't likely to now, either.

10

'Hi, *you*! Who do you think you're staring at? There was no response, so the speaker tried again. 'I *said* – who are you staring at?'

Adam hadn't been staring at anyone. A group of boys from Greys College – four or five of them – stood at the edge of the Green, all in their purple school uniform. One of the boys was taller than the others and wore a different coloured tie.

The tall one shouted again. '*You!* Who are you staring at?'

Molly and Adam had been sitting on a bench by the Green in front of Ely Cathedral. They were waiting for Abigail, who had gone to the dentist. Molly was reading *Jane Eyre*, and Adam's attention had been arrested by the great cannon that stood on the grass. He quickly sketched the outlines of a picture, with the cathedral in the background and the ancient gun centre-stage. But it would be more interesting, he thought, if the cannon was aimed *at* the cathedral instead of away from it.

He'd walked across to take a closer look. Molly, hardly noticing, continued to read her book.

Purple-Blazer walked towards Adam. 'When I walk

around the city, I don't expect to be gawped at by oiks!'

Adam pulled a face. 'What's an oik?' he asked.

'*You* are!' Purple-Blazer retorted. 'You're a common-or-garden oik!'

He waited for Adam's reply but got none. 'I dislike oiks!' he said then.

Adam raised his eyebrows slightly. That was Purple-Blazer's problem, not his.

'Well?'

'Well what?' Adam said.

'Aren't you going to fight me?'

'Why should I?'

'I called you an oik.'

Adam shrugged. He found it hard to play his required part in this ritual.

'Perhaps,' Purple-Blazer went on, 'you are a *coward* as well as an oik!'

Adam glanced back at Molly, who had laid down her book and was recovering her awareness of what was happening around her.

Purple-Blazer removed his purple blazer and dropped it loosely on the grass. He stared at Adam. 'Aren't you going to take yours off?' he demanded.

'Is that one of the rules?' Adam asked.

'It's a gentlemanly sort of thing to do,' Purple-Blazer said. His friends drew closer to him, in support, but he waved them away imperiously. 'Leave this to me!' he said.

'I don't think I'll bother,' Adam said.

Purple-Blazer walked forward and took up a position facing Adam. He stood with one foot advanced and both fists raised menacingly in front of him.

'Well?' Purple-Blazer said.

Adam ignored his opponent's posture and just hit his head – hard – with his right fist. The blow landed smack in the middle of Purple-Blazer's face. He took several staggered steps backwards, then collapsed on the grass.

An elderly man in clerical dress hurried nervously away. And Adam registered the fact that when a fist composed mostly of bone encounters a head also made of bone, *both* get hurt.

Molly ran across the grass towards them, leaving *Jane Eyre* on the bench. Adam, with a look of injured surprise on his face, massaged his fist while she attended to Purple-Blazer where he lay groaning on the grass. Blood was pouring from the left side of his nose and there was a cut below his left eye.

Perhaps he lost consciousness for a moment or two. As he came round Purple-Blazer seemed to become dizzily aware that a girl was kneeling on the grass beside him. She had the loveliest face he'd ever seen.

There was a limit to Molly's compassion: she *would* have used her own hankie to wipe Purple-Blazer's disgustingly bloody face, but when she saw his protruding from his shirt pocket, she pulled it out and used that.

'Can you walk?' she said.

'I think so,' Purple-Blazer said slowly.

'Well, stand up then,' Molly said crossly.

Although he'd been punched in the face, Purple-Blazer seemed to have developed a limp. He put one arm around Molly's shoulder and allowed her to support him to the bench where she had left *Jane Eyre*.

Adam picked up the purple blazer and followed sheepishly.

They sat on the bench, side by side, with Molly in the middle.

'Your friends have scarpered,' Adam said to Purple-Blazer.

Purple-Blazer didn't seem to mind much. 'They're a useless lot,' he said. Then he turned to Molly and said, 'Who are you?' He sounded as if he were drunk, but that was the effect of Adam's blow.

'I'm an oik,' Molly snapped. 'A *female* oik!'

Adam had opened his sketchbook again and Purple-Blazer stared blearily at it across the front of Molly. He leaned heavily on her knee and jabbed a finger sharply down on Adam's drawing.

'I say! That's *jolly* good!' he said.

Adam was opening and closing his right hand, wondering if he'd ever draw again.

'Thing *is*,' Purple-Blazer went on, 'you've drawn the bally gun the wrong way round!' He peered up at Adam, blearily bloody, confused, but not unfriendly.

Abigail, returning from the dentist and wiping dribble from her paralysed mouth, said slowly, 'Whoff going on?'

11

Abigail was troubled by suspicions about Ivy. One evening, she tackled her.

'Ivy?'

'What?'

'Who was your mum?'

'Who was my mum? What sort of question is *that*? You *know* who my mum was!'

Yes, Abigail thought, *the woman I called Auntie Sheila – who wore no wedding ring and lived alone.*

Ivy looked pityingly at the two younger girls. 'I know what you're thinking,' she said. 'What you really wanted to ask was: who was my *dad*? Well,' she said slowly, emphasising each word, '*my – mum – never – married – my – dad*, that's all. It *happens*! Even in Great Deeping it must happen sometimes! You two are so *young*!'

So Abigail asked her mum about it. 'Did you know Ivy's father?' she said.

Mrs Murfitt was pushing a carpet-sweeper backwards and forwards over the living room floor. 'Yes, I did,' she said. 'Nasty bit of work, he was!'

She stopped and leaned on the handle of the carpet-sweeper. 'I used to go and stay at Sheila's. In the school holidays. There was a man there, a neighbour. Quite a bit older than Sheila.'

She stopped, as if hoping that explained everything. 'Sheila was . . .' She paused. '. . . in love with him. At least, she thought she was. And he said he loved her.'

'What happened?'

'What do you *think* happened? She had a baby. She called the baby Ivy.'

'Wasn't she too young?'

'She was sixteen. Fifteen when the baby started.'

Fifteen! The same age as us! Abigail thought.

'He denied the baby was anything to do with him. Why would he be interested in a school kid, he said. Everyone believed him. And soon afterwards, he left home.'

'And Auntie Sheila kept the baby?'

'What choice did she have? So the baby was brought up as Ivy Westgate. If Sheila had married him, she'd have been Ivy Winters.'

Mrs Murfitt straightened up to resume the carpet sweeping. 'I was never allowed to go there again! My mum thought I might be corrupted by such wicked goings-on.'

On a fine March morning, Adam sat in the sun on a bench in the tiny garden behind his art teacher's studio.

Mrs Fraser sat beside him on the bench. After a few

moments she said in her low voice, 'Adam, would you let me buy one of your drawings?'

'*Buy?*' No one had ever bought any of his work.

'This one,' she said.

She held in her hand a pen-and-ink-and-watercolour drawing of the inside of the studio. In it, she was working at her easel and her husband was leaning over his printing press.

'Why this one?'

She smiled slowly, in the way she sometimes did. 'The line work is very mature,' she said. 'Would you accept five pounds?'

Five pounds!

'I would buy *all* his drawings,' Molly said to Abigail later, 'if I had any money.'

'He would *give* you all his drawings if you asked for them,' said Abigail. 'You know he would.'

12

A neighbour had found an unwanted child-seat for a bicycle and given it to Mrs Barnes. Adam had fixed it to the back of her old bone-shaker. So, when one cold Saturday afternoon they decided to cycle to Ely, young William was able to go too. He rode high and proud, huddled from the bitter wind behind Adam's back.

They wandered around the market, made a tour of Woolworth's and free-wheeled down Fore Hill to the river side. It was a shabby, run-down area and the fat wide river was dark and forbidding. A railway bridge crossed it and the waterside footpath went under the bridge. Here, to their surprise, they came across Purple-Blazer and three of his purple-blazered friends.

'Oh, *no!*' Molly said. She feared another punch-up.

The boys appeared to be having an argument. But when he saw them approaching, Purple-Blazer turned and shouted a greeting.

'Oiks ahoy!' he called cheerfully.

'So they've let you out – *again!*' Adam said. 'Shouldn't you all be safely tucked up in your dormitories?'

Purple-Blazer put on a haughty look. 'This is no joke,'

he said. 'We're here to put Gulliver through his ordeal.'

'Gulliver?' said Molly.

'Ordeal?' said Abigail.

'It's one of our traditions. Everyone in my House has to do it. And Gulliver is funking it.'

'What does he have to do?'

'He has to swing from girder to girder across the river under the railway bridge, using his hands. Then he has to swing back again. There's nothing to it.'

'It's all very well for you,' Gulliver said. 'I can't swim.'

'You should jolly well have learned last summer,' Purple-Blazer said. 'Everyone else did.'

Molly could foresee how this situation might develop. 'Come on,' she said to Adam. 'It's time we got going.'

But Adam was interested. The railway bridge was made of huge steel girders. It cast a cold shadow over the river at an oblique angle. This side, the river path went under the bridge, but on the other side there was no path. Just a damp brick wall rising straight out of the water.

'Have *you* done it?' Adam asked Purple-Blazer.

'Of course.' Molly recognised the tone. Haughty, self-confident, indignant at such a doubt. 'Three times,' Purple-Blazer added.

But Gulliver was firm. He was not going to risk drowning by hanging over the river under that bridge. 'Well, I call that a jolly bad show!' Purple-Blazer said.

Then he brightened up. 'I say! Why don't *you* have a

go?' he said to Adam. 'Show us what you're made of.'

Molly's heart sank.

Just in case Adam hadn't understood, Purple-Blazer made it explicit. 'I tell you what! I'll challenge you,' he said. 'If I had a gauntlet, I'd throw it at your feet.'

'And if Adam had any sense he'd throw it right back at you!' Abigail said.

But the girls were irrelevant. Purple-Blazer was serious about this.

'All right,' Adam said calmly. 'If you show me what to do.'

'Of course! I'll come with you. An officer should never ask his men to do something he's not prepared to do himself.'

'You're not my officer,' Adam said.

'I might be – one day.'

Officer or not, it was Adam who took charge. 'This is what we'll do,' he said.

Purple-Blazer showed his surprise. But he listened as Adam explained. 'We'll go across – *together* – so that you can show me how to do it.'

'Then what?'

'We'll *race* back. From the other side.'

'What's the prize?' one of the purple-blazers asked.

No one could think of a prize. Then the littlest of them suggested a forfeit for the loser instead of a prize for the winner.

'Jolly good wheeze, Shawcross Minor!' Purple-Blazer said. 'But what?'

The boys all pondered. Molly walked a few paces away from this nonsense. Then young Shawcross came up with an idea. 'The loser has to take a day trip to London.'

'To get killed by a V-2, I suppose,' Abigail said.

'Not necessarily,' Shawcross Minor said.

'It's not such a big risk,' Adam said. 'People *live* in London.'

'And people go there to work every day,' young Shawcross pointed out. '*You'd* only be going once.' His own family lived near Hampstead Heath.

'It's not much of a forfeit,' Purple-Blazer said doubtfully. 'It's a treat, really.'

'No, it isn't. Because you have to go on a school day.'

That put a different complexion on the whole idea. Playing truant was a serious matter. 'When?' Purple-Blazer said quietly.

'Monday?'

'No,' Purple-Blazer said firmly. 'House rugger finals.'

'Tuesday then.'

Molly sighed at the stupidity of all this. But Adam just said 'OK.'

Then Abigail intervened. 'We don't know any of your names,' she said.

'Fair point,' Purple-Blazer said. 'I'm Macaulay.'

'No,' Abigail said. 'Your *first* name.'

'We don't go in for first names at Greys,' Purple-Blazer said loftily.

But Abigail insisted. She'd found a weak point in

their armour-plating – they found first names embarrassing. Purple-Blazer was actually blushing.

'Mine is Hamish,' he said unwillingly. 'Hamish Macaulay.' He spoke as if it hurt.

Anyone would think we'd asked him to take his trousers off! Abigail said to Molly afterwards.

'Haw-haw-haw!' Gulliver mocked. '*Hamish!*'

'And Gulliver's first name is Turlington,' Hamish said sternly. '*Turlington* Gulliver.'

It was impossible not to smile, however hard they tried. 'Mine's Harrison,' young Shawcross said eagerly. 'Harrison Corcoran Shawcross.'

'What about him?' Abigail indicated the fourth member of the group, a rather pleasant-looking boy, but silent.

'I'm Whittington Mudd,' he said, blushing.

'Is Whittington your first name?'

He shook his head. 'There's a hyphen,' he said.

Molly hoped Whittington-Mudd's first name would be a sensible one. 'Charles,' he said. 'Charles Whittington-Mudd.' That was all right. There was no need to be embarrassed about a name like Charles. But it might have been Algernon, Molly thought. Or Mungo.

'I'm Adam,' Adam said.

'The first man,' Hamish murmured, almost to himself. But Molly heard – and she warmed to him a little because he'd said that.

'Adam what?'

'Adam Swales.'

Then the female oiks revealed their names. There was no embarrassment about that. The boys from Greys College expected girls to have first names.

Now the race could start. Hamish climbed up the grassy bank to where he could reach the girders overhead. Then he took hold. Adam followed him and reached up. The grip was not much more than an inch-and-a-half wide.

Both boys swung by their finger-ends and edged out over the path. 'Got it?' Hamish asked.

Adam had – but only just. The hard rusty metal gave very little purchase and already his fingers were hurting. He took one hand off and moved it along, but with his whole weight concentrated on only four fingers, the pain was worse.

The two boys edged out over the riverside path, and then the Great Ouse was under them. It was a deep and powerful river – black in the cavernous shadows under the bridge, sliding glassily sea-wards.

'Can you swim?' Hamish asked.

'Yes,' Adam gasped back. They both knew that swimming wouldn't be any good, fully-dressed, in that black and bitter water. He'd be washed half a mile downstream before anyone could get help.

He discovered a rhythm for his movements and managed to keep up with Hamish. They swung sideways, facing each other. Adam's mind was entirely focused on his fingertips. He imagined them bleeding and raw.

On the far side there was no pathway where they

might take a rest. Molly watched anxiously as they hung for a few seconds, motionless. 'One of you girls start us off,' Hamish called across the river. His voice was cramped and breathless.

So Abigail shouted *ready, steady, GO!* – and the boys started on the return crossing, racing now. They heard a freight train approaching from Ely station, heaving its hundreds of tons and thundering just over their heads. The wheels clattered der-*dung* der-*dung*. The unbearable noise would go on for ages, forty or fifty trucks perhaps, echoing and magnified in this cold metallic underworld.

Adam realised he had drawn ahead slightly. An advantage of a few inches only. He wasn't worried about paying the forfeit; he just wanted to *win*. The end of the goods train passed over at last, clattering off into the distance. And in the silence nothing could be heard but the soft slopping of the river and the rasping breath of the two boys.

The pain in his finger-ends no longer troubled Adam. It was the ache along his arms and behind his shoulders. He imagined muscular tendons snapping with the strain. And his neck hurt with the constant looking up. Each swinging movement gave one hand and one arm a brief rest while the other did the work. Then they swapped. Pain and rest, turn-about and turn-about.

Adam won, by about six inches. He dropped down at Molly's feet, gasping and massaging his fingers.

Hamish followed a second or so later. 'Jolly well done!' he said. He was generous in defeat.

Gulliver turned his attention to young William. '*You* never told us *your* name,' he said.

He began to ask questions – silly questions like 'Whose ickle brother are *you*, then?' And, when he got no answer, 'Whose ickle *sister* are you?'

The little boy stood still, silent and frightened. Gulliver bent down in front of him and tapped his knuckles on William's forehead. '*Is there anybody there? said the traveller.*'

He looked back over his shoulder at the others, inviting them to laugh. Then he knocked on William's forehead again. '*Is there anybody there?*' he said.

There was a brief stupefied silence. Hamish was the first to react. He cuffed Gulliver on the side of his head, not hard enough to hurt him, but strongly enough to tip him over sideways onto the grass. 'You're a slimy toad, Gulliver!' he said. 'The boy's probably got more sense than you'll ever have.'

Gulliver, sprawling on the ground, muttered something – certainly not an apology.

Molly and Abigail – both outraged – did nothing. Partly because Hamish had done it for them, and partly because both had looked at Adam. His face was white with fury.

'I don't allow bullying in my House,' Hamish said.

'*He's* not in our House,' Gulliver protested. 'He's not even at our school!'

'But *you* are! I can beat you for this and I probably *will.*'

13

Somewhere in south-east London, over two cups of Camp coffee, a battle was taking place. Only a small one, just a battle of words. But nasty.

Frosty started it. 'About Willy Wilson,' he said.

The Maggot gave him a funny look. '*What* about him?'

'I went to his funeral.'

'So?'

'I didn't see *you* there.'

'That's because I *wasn't* there.'

'There weren't no flowers neither,' Frosty said.

'Were there many people?'

Frosty was sarcastic. 'Oh, yeah! *Three*, including me.'

'Who were the other two?'

'Coppers.' (*That'll* worry him!, Frosty thought.)

But the Maggot didn't look worried. Often when he was with Frosty he would peer up into his face with interest, as if he was amused. Or puzzled. Almost as if he was Frosty's father. Frosty didn't like it. It unnerved him.

'Did you talk to 'em?' the Maggot asked.

'Of course I talked to 'em.'

'What did you tell 'em?'

'The troof.' (That was daring of Frosty, making fun of the way the Maggot talked.)

'How much of the troof?' (Stirring his coffee.)

'Enough.' (Make the blighter worried.)

'*Enough for what, Frosty?*' The amused look of interest was gone. This was menacing, eye-to-eye, the coffee spoon motionless in the Maggot's hand.

'Enough to keep 'em happy.' (Scared. Backing down.)

'Drink your coffee, Frosty! Or are you worried it's been poisoned?'

(It might be, Frosty thought unhappily.)

Another defeat. Poor old Frosty! As he walked away he remembered what Jimmy Riddle had said about Willy. *He was marked, mate. Neatly marked!*

14

Early on Tuesday morning, Hamish Macaulay stood in the waiting room at Ely station, waiting for the London train. As it pulled in, windows were lowered, purple-sleeved arms reached out, door handles were turned, and carriage doors swung open.

Twenty or thirty pupils from Greys College streamed out onto the platform.

They were day-pupils, an inferior race.

Nevertheless, Hamish had no wish to be seen by them. So he hesitated inside the waiting room. Then, to his surprise, he saw there was a boy on the train, wearing a grammar school uniform and holding open a door almost opposite him.

It was Adam – who had seen Hamish's difficulty at once. He shouted at the top of his voice – 'I say! *Look!*' – and pointed to the sky above the engine at the front of the train.

Everyone on the platform peered first at the boy who had shouted, and then upwards to see what he was pointing at.

Hamish saw his chance. He dashed across the platform and on to the train.

'What are *you* doing here?' he said to Adam. And as he climbed aboard he saw that the girl was there too. 'Checking up on me, are you?' he said. 'Making sure I pay my forfeit?'

'No,' Adam said equably. 'It's just that you shouldn't expect a person to do something you wouldn't do yourself.'

Hamish was surprised to find that he was pleased to see them, *very* pleased in fact. He sat next to Adam, facing Molly so that he could look at her. He didn't get many chances to look at girls close up.

But why, Hamish wondered, had she decided to come too?

It was her father. It was because of *him* that Molly took off to London with Adam that day.

He'd had a weekend leave and he'd talked non-stop about his plans for the Deeping Hotel. It had been fun, exciting – until he mentioned in passing how he himself would deal with the bookings, her mum would run the kitchen, and Molly would look after the rooms and supervise the cleaning.

'But I won't be here,' Molly had said.

Her dad was outraged. She wanted to go *where*? *University*? Two extra years at school to take Highers? What on earth *for*? Then another three years on top of that? He'd never heard such nonsense! She could stay at school one more year to take her School Cert – and then she would leave and start to earn her keep. She should feel grateful.

'Adam won't be leaving at sixteen.'

That was a mistake. Her father looked as if the light of understanding was dawning. 'Oh,' he said. 'It's *him* we have to thank for this crazy idea.'

And her mother had sided with him! They'd been together all through the War, she and her mum, looking after her younger brother and running the not-very-successful guesthouse. Her father was an outsider coming back into their lives. Not just an outsider, an *intruder!*

No one in their family, Mr Barnes said, had ever stayed at school beyond the age of fourteen. Molly should think herself lucky. She was to say no more about it.

That had happened on Sunday night. So when Adam told her on Monday that he intended to go to London with Hamish Macaulay – and did she want to go too? – she hadn't hesitated. Smarting with injustice, she said yes, she *would*.

Hamish had bought a copy of the *News Chronicle*. 'It's very good news,' he said. Allied forces advancing into Germany, the headline said. American and British troops had crossed the Rhine and were driving back the weakened German army. Meanwhile the Russians were advancing through Poland and Czechoslovakia.

'*This is the final drive into the heart of Germany,*' Hamish read. '*Victory is at last within sight.*'

'It will soon be over,' Molly said. It was easy to say but difficult to grasp. People had been saying *when the War is over* for most of her remembered life. Soon it really would be. 'What will they do to Hitler when they capture him?' she asked.

'Shoot him,' Adam said.

'Hang him,' said Hamish.

Neither of them cared how it was done.

'Is your father in the War?' Molly asked Hamish.

'Not any more.'

Molly had learned from experience that it was better to ask directly, without embarrassment. 'Is he dead?' she said.

But Hamish's father wasn't dead. 'He *was* fighting in Burma. But now he's in a Japanese POW camp.'

He changed the subject. 'I say! I've got some super tuck! Want some?'

He took from his satchel a truly enormous parcel. 'I persuaded Mrs Marston, our cook. I'm a favourite of hers. Help yourselves.'

'We are the most ginormous duffers, you know,' he said cheerfully as he munched. 'There'll be a truly everestine fuss when everyone finds out.'

'*Everestine*?'

'It's one of our sayings at Greys,' he explained. 'Mount Everest. *You* know! Something jolly big!'

'All the more reason then,' Molly said, 'to make the

most of today.' Molly warmed to her idea. 'We mustn't just mooch about London for a few hours and then come back again. We have to *do* something.'

They agreed that each of them would choose one place to visit and they would go together to all three places.

London was tired and shabby, with bombsites overgrown with nettles, brambles and buddleia bushes. It was a sad grey place that day, and Mr Swales had been right – you could tell that the people were tired and fed-up. The buzzbombs were bad enough, with their ten seconds of silence. But then the V-2s had started – and they were worse.

A second blitz, people called it.

Adam had known immediately where he wanted to go. He took them across central London to a quiet street close to the north bank of the Thames. Here they found what Adam wanted to see. A small, rather elegant, shop. *Paterson Royce – Fine Art Dealer.*

'He comes to see my art teacher,' he explained. 'And he's supposed to be interested in my drawings. *I* think he's an idiot.'

Hamish and Molly peered into the window of the gallery, amateurs, not knowing quite what they were looking for. But Adam wanted to see what Paterson Royce sold in his art gallery, and what prices he charged.

'*Golly!*'

The window was criss-crossed with sticky tape in case of damage from broken glass. But they could clearly see what was on display – a couple of oil paintings, a few watercolours and a white statuette of a woman with a cat. But most of the items were black-and-white drawings. Five were clearly labelled by Picasso.

The prices of the drawings astonished Molly and Hamish. The cheapest was £5 – an extraordinary price, they thought. That was a week's wages! One was £75!

'What's so special about that one?' Hamish asked Adam.

'It's an original drawing. The others are prints.'

It was hard to see the difference; both were crisp and clear, done in black line.

'I say,' Hamish remarked. 'You'll be jolly rich one day, if you can draw like that.'

'He can,' Molly said proudly.

Then it was Molly's turn to choose where to go. This was easy: she just wanted to see Westminster Abbey, the Houses of Parliament and Big Ben. In Downing Street, they wondered if they might get a glimpse of Mr Churchill. But no such luck.

They crossed Trafalgar Square and walked past the National Gallery, empty of pictures. Up Charing Cross Road they went, three cheerful tourists, companionable and unhurried.

Hamish's choice surprised them. He collected old coins, he said. There was a shop in Bedford Square that specialised in them. On their way they stopped at a café in Tottenham Court Road and had a snack. The *Barrel of Beef* it was called, a tiny place, crowded and cheerful, cramped in a basement at the bottom of a block of offices.

Outside, Hamish led them away, towards Bedford Square.

The eastern sky was quietly sliced, the tender layers of cloud briefly creased. There was something in the air, a brief flicker. Only Adam noticed.

There was a sharp flash of blue light and an explosion that shook the hearts out of them. There was a boom like an earthquake, an ugly lump of sound, and the ground shook under their feet. Looking back, they saw the *Barrel of Beef* where they'd had their snack – along with the floors above it and the next-door buildings – erupting. Upwards first, as if pushed from underground, then outwards, collapsing into a huge obliterating cloud of dust. Tables, chairs, cookers, people, a million pathetic fragments.

There was a bang, meaningless, somewhere high up. And the sound of something approaching in the sky, screaming.

None of it made any sense. Shards of broken plate-glass flew through the air and skidded at high speed along the road towards them. With amazing presence of mind Hamish had shoved Adam and Molly into the doorway of the coin shop. A good thing, because glass from the building above them came water-falling down, just missing them. Then a great clattering of débris – tiles, great splinters of timber, monolithic chimneystacks, bricks, worse. Finally, showers of soot, blasted out of nearby chimneys, billowed messily down onto the stunned and silent street.

There was confusion inside the coin shop. The lights had gone out and someone was shouting. A woman came hurrying up the stairs from the basement, calling out for Doug. '*Doug!*' she screamed. '*Doug! Doug!* Oh, Dougie, where are you? The *lav!* The *lav!*'

She rushed towards the door. The back of her skirt was caught up in her knickers. 'The *lav!* I was sitting on the lavvy and it cracked in two right under me,' she screamed. It was Molly she was telling. 'It broke in two just as I was starting . . . Oh, *Doug!*'

Douglas emerged from somewhere inside. 'Mavis, darlin', it's OK. We're OK.' He spoke gently, put his arms round her and shushed her away, inside. 'We can get a new lav.'

The three of them moved out into the street to take in the desolation – shocked people blown sideways, bleeding from head wounds, staggering to lean on the nearest wall. Molly for some reason crouched down on her heels, her hands clutched at her mouth and leaning her shoulder sideways against one of the boys. She was half aware that one of them – Adam? – had his hand on her head.

The frozen tableau came to life. There were shouts and cries for help. Incredibly, people were appearing from the buildings closest to the crater – dazed, white-faced, pushing back their dust-encrusted hair. Already there was a fire engine and a fire officer was beginning to organise the rescue operation.

'We must help,' Hamish said. His voice sounded thick. Dumbly Molly followed the boys towards the centre of the chaos. But an Air Raid Warden turned them back. 'Best leave this to us as is trained for it,' he said.

They never got to see inside the coin shop. They decided to go straight to Liverpool Street and go home. Molly felt sweaty and sick. That's fear, Hamish told her, and he was probably right: she knew she wouldn't feel safe until their train was out of London.

The train reached Great Deeping late in the afternoon, so that they got home at their usual school time. They told no one what had happened, except Abigail.

Molly expected the night would be full of nightmares. But she slept deeply. The next day, however, she was troubled by an impossible memory – a red double-decker bus lifted off the ground, blasted over on to its side and overwhelmed by huge chunks of falling brickwork, engulfing its passengers. It was a number 73, and as it was crushed a hand was stuck out of an upstairs window, waving.

Molly never had any troubled nights about what had happened. But, for years, the memory of the bus lurked

77

in the basement of her mind. At any time, it would come unbidden into her thoughts as she went about her daily business, an insistent picture, with a bright and vivid clarity.

The forfeits had to be paid. Playing truant was a serious matter.

Hamish came off worst. He was closely questioned by both his headmaster and housemaster. Next morning after prayers, he was rebuked in front of the whole school – lectured, humiliated, disgraced, and ordered to come forward and hand in his prefect's badge and tie. He had disgraced his house, his school, his family, his king and country. Almost high treason.

In silence, as everyone watched, he returned to his seat, tieless, stubbornly unembarrassed.

Adam too was questioned. After assembly the headmaster gave the whole school a lecture on Responsibility. Everyone – from the deputy head to the tiniest boy in the front row – was wondering if Adam Swales would be caned. The possibility fascinated them. For some reason no one could imagine Swalesy bending over a chair and submitting to such a thing. Easier to imagine *him* caning the headmaster.

But no. Mr Ricks took a strict line on truancy, but he was less agitated about it than Hamish's head. Other evacuee boys at the grammar school occasionally took off and went back to London. So there was to be no caning. But Adam was required that evening to write a thousand times *I must retain my self-respect by not playing truant*. A thousand! Everyone was outraged.

Molly got off scot-free.

At registration, when Molly's name had been called, Abigail answered for her. If their form-mistress had taught English or Maths or History, it wouldn't have worked. The teacher would have spotted the empty desk when she came to teach the class. But their form-mistress taught R.S., one period a week, on Thursdays.

So Molly's empty place went unnoticed. In any case, Thursday was the last day of term. The day after that was Good Friday. So Molly paid no forfeit.

That was the last bomb to fall on London in World War 2. Somewhere in Europe the advancing allied army found the last rocket-launcher and immobilised it. So no more V-2 rockets fell on London, or anywhere else.

It was over. The V-1s had stopped a week or two earlier. And now there were no more bombing raids, no more landmines, no more incendiaries.

It had come to an end, as all bad things do finally. One way or the other.

Now, jump ahead a few years. To London again, but more than sixty years later. Not in Tottenham Court

Road this time, but just round the corner, in Oxford Street.

London has long ago healed itself, rebuilt its ruins and grown another skin.

It's a sunny spring morning in 2006, and an old lady is stepping carefully from a red London bus. She is Molly Barnes, and with her is a girl, about ten years old, perhaps eleven.

'*Look!* That's him!' the girl says excitedly. She is pointing.

They are approaching a private art gallery where a new exhibition is soon to open, celebrating the work of Adam Swales. There are posters, with his face. It's a well-known image; the original is in the National Portrait Gallery.

Molly and her young companion enter the gallery. The automatic doors nudge softly together behind them and the sounds of the street are sliced into silence. A worried young woman approaches them, with a mobile phone in her hand and dark glasses pushed up in her hair. 'Professor Barnes?' she asks.

'Yes. I've come for an interview.' I sound like someone applying for a job, Molly thinks. 'With the BBC,' she adds. 'For the *Art Today* programme. This is my granddaughter.'

Molly looks around, taking it all in. Everywhere there is a brightness, and people quietly moving through pale galleries. They talk softly, and their feet are noiseless on the white wooden floor. There is a quiet unhurried busyness in the cool brightness, with no one fussing. Molly is impressed.

'Your interview is to be in Gallery One,' the young woman says.

A sign says *Gallery One ~ Wartime and Childhood.* Molly stares at the drawings, moving her eyes slowly along the walls, remembering.

When the crowds come, Molly thinks, this is what they'll see – Adam's drawings tastefully framed and well behaved.

Unlike Adam.

She is overwhelmed by longing.

15

Molly had no idea how strong a man could be, no notion of the hard muscularity a man could call upon. Until the moment she was seized, she had not been so enclosed by another human body since she'd been a small child.

They had always scoffed at the idea of someone lurking and they were convinced of their absolute safety. Adam could look after himself, and, as for Molly, *she* was the fastest runner in Great Deeping. Every year at the annual sports, she won the 100 yards, the 220 and the 440. She never trained or practised; she just ran – *fast*.

She was on her way, later than usual, to Abigail's house. Foolish, she knew, to go alone through the blacked-out streets, but she'd done it hundreds of times and she'd never come to any harm. It was a dark still night. The houses on the left-hand side opened directly onto the street, and there was one set back an extra three feet or so, creating a dark corner. Here, a telegraph pole stood, forming an additional corner behind it – an intensified hiding place. As she hurried past, she heard a breath taken behind her and a movement.

In that brief instant she had known at once what was going to happen.

His strength was terrifying and there was no escaping the relentless hardness of his grip. His right hand was across her mouth, unmovable and suffocating, like iron. His other arm was clamped around her chest so that both her arms were trapped. There could be no escape, no protest. Molly kicked backwards, but she failed to make contact.

'*Molly!*'

Molly went still at once, every particle of her body attentive.

'Molly, *listen!*'

That voice! Did she recognise it?

'I want to talk to you for a minute. I'll let go if you promise not to run away. And not to scream. *Please!* I won't hurt you!'

You *are* hurting me! she thought wildly.

Her head was paralysed in his grip, but she managed to move it enough to indicate *yes*. For a moment, nothing. Perhaps he was thinking. Then he moved his hands, put them quickly on her shoulders and turned her round to face him.

She had half-known his voice, now she almost recognised his face. But it couldn't be! It just could not be. The last time she'd seen him, her face had been level with his stomach. Now she was at his height, looking him in the eye. Sharp eyes they were, in a weary ragged face, unshaven and dark.

'Don't you know me, Molly?'

Molly gasped for breath. She did know him – but she couldn't recall who he was.

'I'm Abigail's dad.'

'*Mr Murfitt?*'

'Yes,' he said, with a deep thankful sigh, as if that *yes* closed the curtain on some tense drama.

'Everybody thinks you're dead.' Molly's mind was highly charged and working at great speed. *Has he deserted?* she thought. *Where has he been hiding all this time?*

'I know. But, as you can see . . . '

'Nobody's heard from you for years!'

He nodded. '1940,' he said.

But Mr Murfitt hadn't time to match Molly's emotional pace. 'Listen,' he said. 'I shouldn't be here. If I'm seen, I'll be in trouble. But I just *have* to see Abigail and her mum! I'll go crazy if I don't!'

Inside, Molly was growing angry. Why had he frightened her like that? Why hadn't he just gone straight to the house?

'I want you to do something. *Two* things,' he said.

'What things?' She was suspicious, on her guard.

'If there's anyone else there, I want you to come out and tell me.'

'There won't be anyone else there,' Molly said.

'Good. But promise to come and warn me if there is.'

Molly nodded. 'All right,' she said.

'And I want you to prepare them. Tell them I'm out here. If I just burst in on them . . . '

Part of Molly's mind started thinking ahead at once to what she should say, how she should tell them.

'There's something else. Who's that young woman who's living there now? She's too grown up to be an evacuee.'

'She's some sort of niece,' Molly said. 'Ivy – Ivy Westgate. But she's not there tonight. She's gone to the pictures in Downham. She won't be back till after eleven.'

Then it dawned on her. *'You're the Lurker*! You've been watching the house!'

But Mr Murfitt was distracted. 'Ivy?' he said. 'What's *she* doing here?'

Molly had had enough of this. 'I'm going!' she said, and broke away from him.

He followed her, a few paces behind, part of the darkness. But Molly couldn't endure to walk like that, so she shot off at a pace she knew he wouldn't be able to match and in no time at all she was at Abigail's garden gate. She rushed in, heard it slam behind her. Then she was at the door. She felt her way through the dark scullery, then hurried across the kitchen and pushed open the door of Abigail's living room.

They were sitting at the table, doing a jigsaw puzzle. Mrs Murfitt straightened her shoulders, and Abigail looked up, bright-faced.

Describing it to her mother later, Molly couldn't conceal her bewilderment. 'They didn't seem pleased to see him at all!' she said.

'You shouldn't have stayed.'

'I know. But they asked me to. I left them alone, though. I went in the kitchen and fried some sausages for him, with eggs and baked beans.'

'But why weren't they *pleased to see him*?' she continued. She sat at the kitchen table, baffled, with her chin on her hands. A rule had been broken. Returning soldiers should be greeted with joy. It was obvious, everyone knew that. There were popular songs about it and adverts with happy pictures of reunited families. When the War finally came to an end, that would happen to thousands of families all over the world. A massive multiple happy ending, worldwide.

Mrs Barnes sighed at the complexity of it all. 'Molly, they've both spent five years getting used to the fact that he was almost certainly dead and then he just walks in!'

'But it looked as if they didn't want him there! They looked *angry* – both of them! It was three quarters of an hour before they showed any signs of welcome!'

'Were *you* pleased to see him?'

'No, of course not. He scared me!'

'Perhaps he scared them too,' Mrs Barnes said. Then she added, 'You're not the world's best cook, Molly. Did he enjoy your fry-up?'

'He was starving,' Molly said.

Abigail had joined Molly in the kitchen, to help.

'Aren't you happy?' Molly whispered.

'But where's he *been* all this time? What's he been *doing*?' Her face was pale and the hand that turned over the fried bread was shaking.

Later, after he'd eaten, Mr Murfitt provided some sort of account, the barest hints of a story.

'After Dunkirk, I got left behind. I was wounded – not badly, but I couldn't keep up with the rest. So I dropped out and hid in some farm buildings. For days after that the whole area was overrun with German troops.'

He kept stopping to think. It seemed to Molly that he'd never told this story before and this was the first time he'd thought about it.

'I got taken in by a local family. They kept me hidden and looked after me.'

'Weren't they taking a risk?' Mrs Murfitt said.

'If I'd been found, they'd have been shot – all of them, children as well.'

Would *we* have done that if we'd been invaded? Molly wondered.

'I moved from one family to another, further inland. I got drawn into helping the French resistance. Recruited, really, I suppose.'

'Did the army know? The British army, I mean.'

'Eventually they did. The Secret Intelligence lot. I'm

not supposed to talk about it. They were happy for me to stay there, behind enemy lines.'

'But what did you actually *do*?'

'I was part of an escape network. I helped a few of our men to get home – airmen mostly, who had been shot down. Later, I started to get information back to our side.'

Mr Murfitt paused, perhaps wondering how much he could tell them. 'You know about the V-1s? The doodlebugs? Well, the Germans were developing that by 1942. Secret Intelligence needed to know where they were. So that the sites could be bombed. I got involved in that.'

'What was it like?' Abigail asked in a low voice. There were many mysteries in this shadowy story.

Mr Murfitt sat back in his chair and looked around him. 'A bit like this. Sitting in other people's kitchens after dark, eating food, and waiting for a knock on the door.'

No one knocked on Mrs Murfitt's door.

'Michael, it's been *five years*.'

He looked guiltily at his wife then.

'All that time we thought you were dead! Five years! Couldn't we have been told?'

'It wouldn't have been safe. *You* might have been in danger.'

A new question was being defined, too difficult to be asked outright. *Could* he have chosen to escape and come home, if he'd wanted to?

'Then D-Day came. Eventually, our troops liberated my bit of France and I was able to come back to England.'

'But why couldn't he come straight home?' Molly's mum wondered later. 'Why did he have to spend all that time lurking?'

'I don't think he's been lurking all the time,' Molly said. 'He's been on extended leave in London, with orders to stay there. But he couldn't resist coming down to have a look at his house sometimes.'

'I don't understand that,' Mrs Barnes said. 'The War's nearly over. Why do they need to keep him secret still?'

'He thinks they have some more work for him to do,' Molly said miserably.

'It's crazy!' her mum said. 'What's he doing tonight – going into hiding again?'

Molly shook her head. 'He's going to stay one night. But he'll have to be quiet and stay in his bedroom while Ivy's in the house. She mustn't know – she'd tell everyone.'

16

'What've you got, Frosty?'

'Shirts – high quality shirts.'

'Let's have a dekko. They're creased. They've been *worn*!'

'Of course they've been worn! That's the only way they could be got out.'

'They're not bad, not bad at all. Take them to a laundry, Frosty. Then I'll take them off your hands.'

'Smart enough, are they, for your new *clee-on-tell*?'

'Don't be sarky, Frosty. I don't like it.'

It was a crazy April.

That morning it had been as warm as summer. But now, in the early evening, it was snowing thickly. Molly and Abigail knelt at the window in Molly's bedroom, watching. Fat clumps of snow billowed lazily around outside. The sky was black and thunderous.

'Did you read about those concentration camps?'

Abigail nodded. They'd read the newspapers, seen the pictures of Belsen and Buchenwald.

The snowflakes rustled almost inaudibly against the

windowpanes. Molly shivered. Abigail tucked her arm into hers and pushed up close.

The others were downstairs, in Mrs Barnes' big kitchen. Adam and young William. Ivy too. But Abigail had tugged softly at Molly's sleeve and indicated that she wanted to go upstairs. But when they got there Abigail said nothing.

'You used to be the cheerful one,' Molly said bleakly, still looking out at the snow.

Abigail's profile was pale in the snow-light. 'I think I'm turning into someone else,' she said. Then, in an abrupt change of mood, she leapt to her feet. 'Come on! Let's go down and see what the others are doing!'

Downstairs, in the kitchen, Adam was sorting out his drawings. The table was almost covered with them.

'More Spicattoes?' Ivy said.

Adam corrected her. 'Picasso.'

Ivy studied them, baffled by the strange figures. She picked up one that she found funny and – just as Abigail and Molly walked in – she burst into a sudden peel of laughter. They'd never heard her laugh like that – sheer delighted laughter. *Perhaps she's beginning to feel at home at last*, Molly thought hopefully. *What's she up to now?* Abigail wondered.

Mr Whymper was there that evening and in a rare burst of friendliness had agreed to show William his postcards. Not his proper collection – that was safely locked in his bedroom. But he had a box of spares and duplicates. 'You can have some of these,' he said to the little boy, 'if there are any you like.'

William loved them. There were pictures of sea-fronts, public gardens, and promenades with trams. It was a lost world from before the War. Abigail and Molly thought Mr Whymper was weird and they steered clear of him if they could, but William liked him. Perhaps it was because he was a quiet man.

'Why do you make *copies*?' Ivy exclaimed to Adam. 'Copy, copy, copy! They're *forgeries*!'

Adam just smiled briefly. It was Molly, as usual, who tried to put Ivy straight. 'They're not forgeries. He's not going to sell them and pretend they're really by Picasso.'

'Huh!'

There was a shout from upstairs. Mrs Barnes was calling to everybody to come up.

Chairs were pushed back as they got to their feet, there was a rush along the dark passage and a great clumping as they all, including Mr Whymper, hurried up the stairs.

Mrs Barnes was in Molly's room. 'Come and see!' she called, and they all crowded in.

'My streetlight!' Molly said.

Outside, no more than a yard from her window, stood the streetlight, *her* streetlight. It had been turned off in September 1939 and had stayed unlit all through the blackout. But Molly remembered how it used to come on dutifully every night at bedtime, softly lighting her room.

'I used to pretend that a family of fairies lived inside it,' she said.

Mrs Barnes opened the window and they crowded at it to peer into the darkening street. There was a cold damp smell of melting snow. About a hundred yards away there was another streetlight. That too was glowing brightly and they could see another beyond that. In the other direction, towards the centre of the town, there were more.

People had their lights lit without closing their shutters or curtains. Someone had opened a front door so that the light fell shamelessly across the wet street. *It's like magic,* Molly thought. *But better than magic, because it's real.*

'It will feel strange, being in bed with the blinds open,' she said. Like being naked, she thought secretly. She was looking forward to it.

Back downstairs, Mr Whymper asked a bold question. He was looking at Adam's Picasso copies. 'Why don't you artists draw things the way they really look?' he said. 'I've never understood that.'

Adam selected a sheet of art paper and a pencil. A silence fell on the room as he drew – and as everyone watched a new Picasso appeared before their eyes. With a confidence and speed which amazed them, Adam drew a window-frame with a streetlight outside, white against the cross-hatched darkness. Inside, seated on a simple chair (a child could draw a better chair than that! Mr Whymper thought), was a girl. She was all circles and loops. Oval face, round shoulders, round breasts, inflated arms, looped-up hair. Only the line of her nose was straight, her mouth shaped, and her eyes and brows firmly sculpted.

No one had ever seen a young woman like that. And yet, unmistakably, it was Molly, sitting alone in her room and mysteriously enjoying her streetlight.

And there *is* the picture, on the wall in Gallery One. It's properly framed now, and it's called *Streetlight*. Seeing it, Molly feels something inexpressibly mysterious and private.

People are arranging television cameras, microphones, lights and screens. A young man with earphones held loosely in one hand turns to Molly and says, 'Professor Barnes?'

She is told where to sit, and where to look. She composes her hands in her lap while a young woman makes up her face.

The young man sits facing her. 'I'm Wigmore,' he says. 'May I check that our background info is correct? You are a Professor at Cambridge University, right?'

'Professor of Archaeology,' Molly says.

'*And* Fellow of St Adelaide's,' her granddaughter adds proudly.

'And you knew Swales when he was a boy?'

Knew him when he was a boy? Molly smiles a little at the dead-fish words. 'He came to live with us in 1940.

He was ten at the time. So was I. He was an evacuee.'

'Most of the stuff in this room was done in 1945,' Wigmore continues. As if Molly didn't know!

'The year the War ended,' Wigmore says.

Yes, *the year the War ended*. To him it is history, Molly thinks sadly. As far as he is concerned, 1945 is not very different from 1845, or 1745. Or 1066 even.

To her, 1945 was the year that she and Adam and Abigail took their first steps into grown-up life, breathing its new air, its new knowledge.

And it was the year that Adam's future had been on a knife-edge.

Literally.

17

In the first week of May, they were all in the kitchen after tea – Mrs Barnes, Mr Barnes (just arrived home on leave and still in uniform), Molly and Adam finishing off their homework, and young William sitting on his father's lap, ready for bed. Their talk was suddenly silenced as they heard a sound outside – someone was leaning a bike against the wall in the backyard.

Footsteps. A hesitation. Then a knock at the door.

Mrs Barnes went to open it. 'Oh!' she said, registering both surprise and puzzlement. In the bright early evening light stood a boy, tall and splendid in a purple school uniform.

'Hello. Is Molly at home, please?'

'Well, yes,' Mrs Barnes said. 'She is.'

Neither of them moved or spoke for a moment. Then the newcomer said, 'I'm Macaulay – Hamish Macaulay.'

Inside, everyone heard this exchange. Adam saw Molly blush, her face, neck, throat. Her whole body, he suspected, right down to her feet.

'I've come to tell Molly the news,' Hamish said. 'I thought she'd be interested to know that Adolf Hitler is dead.'

Mrs Barnes raised her eyebrows ever so slightly. The news of Hitler's death had been broadcast on every wireless network in the world and printed in every newspaper. Everyone had been talking about it all day.

'Do come in,' she said.

Hamish stooped to take off his bicycle clips, then stepped into the kitchen. He saw at once that there was a newspaper on the table. Its front page had the headline: HITLER DEAD – DOENITZ APPOINTED FÜHRER.

'Oh,' Hamish said. 'You knew already.'

Mr Barnes stood William on the floor and rose to greet the guest. He shook hands with Hamish and said he was pleased to meet him. 'You're at Greys?' he asked.

'Yes, sir.'

Mr Barnes wasn't accustomed to being called *sir*. A polite young man, he thought. 'Leaving this summer?' he asked.

'Not this year, sir. I'm in the lower sixth.'

For Mr Barnes, the phrase *lower sixth* suggested a different and privileged world. They had a lower sixth at Molly's school too, and Adam's. But to him it had a whiff of smart young gentlemen in dormitories and common rooms.

'Then university, I suppose?'

'Cambridge, sir.'

'You sound very confident.'

Hamish was modest. 'It's not because I'm clever. It's just that, well, my school has a couple of closed schols at one of the colleges. Only two of us want to go there. So unless I turn out to be a really prize duffer, I ought to get one of them.'

While Molly was wondering what a *schol* was, Mr Barnes changed the subject. 'And what do you think about the death of Hitler?'

Hamish was used to being asked questions like this. His teachers were always doing it and he'd thought about little else all day. 'The trouble is,' he said, 'it won't change anything. A new Führer's been appointed – and he has vowed to fight on.'

Everyone could see that Molly's dad was interested in Hamish. 'Ah,' he said, 'that's as maybe – but he won't be able to fight on.'

'Why not, sir?'

'Because German generals are surrendering all over Europe. In Holland, Norway, Northern Italy. Even in Germany itself a whole army has surrendered.'

Hamish's interest was engaged. This was different. He was talking to a real soldier, not one of his elderly teachers.

'It's over,' Mr Barnes said. 'Take my word for it, Germany's done for. If only we could say the same about the Japs.' Like thousands of allied servicemen in Europe, Molly's dad was afraid that the defeat of the Germans might mean they would all be shipped off to join the fighting in the Far East instead of being demobbed.

'I wondered,' Hamish said, 'if Molly would like to

come for a walk – to discuss Hitler and the War.' He looked at her, a little desperately.

Only young William – who had crawled under the table – knew that Molly's feet were screwed tightly around each other in embarrassment. 'We'll go to see Abigail, if you like,' she said hurriedly. 'I'll get my bike.'

Her mum could not conceal her surprise. 'You never cycle to Abigail's!' she said. It was true. Molly always walked – or ran.

Molly gave her mother a brief angry look. She had no intention of walking through the town with Hamish in his purple school uniform. Apart from other considerations, he might want to hold her hand! She hurried out.

'Will you come?' Hamish said to Adam. But Adam shook his head. 'Physics homework to finish.'

'You two know each other?' Mr Barnes said in surprise.

Hamish smiled. 'Yes. I challenged Adam to a fight.'

'Who won?'

'Oh, Adam did,' Hamish said. 'Fair and square. Knocked me out cold.'

It was clear that Mr Barnes was displeased to hear that.

When Molly arrived outside the back door wheeling her bike, there were some polite goodbyes, and the two of them left.

'Well!' Mrs Barnes said. And then, 'What's a *closed schol*?'

'A *closed scholarship* is the way *rich* people make sure that their *rich* children get the *best* places at the *best* universities.' Mr Barnes' voice was bitter. 'There are – apparently – two of them at this college, reserved for students from Greys. Since no student from another school can get them, the two at Greys are bound to.'

'I thought you rather liked him,' Mrs Barnes said.

'Yes, well . . . That's one of the things that will have to be put a stop to when the War's over.'

Mrs Barnes began to clear away the tea things. Her husband, thoughtful and preoccupied, filled the sink with hot water and tipped in some soapflakes.

'All the same,' he said, 'who would have thought that our Molly would have caught the attention of a young man from Greys?'

18

Word got around that a trainload of prisoners-of-war would be passing through Deeping station on Saturday morning.

A welcome party was arranged to greet them on the platform with cups of tea, cigarettes, perhaps some cakes.

But some people backed away from the idea. What, spend our sugar-coupons on German POWs?

No, not Germans! *British* POWs! – liberated by our armies as they advanced across Europe. They were being flown back to airfields all over the country. In their thousands! Mr Churchill had given orders that every prisoner had to be flown home within twenty-four hours of being freed.

'But will they be . . . *you* know . . . *clean*?'

'They've all been deloused and thoroughly fumigated, madam. There'll be no Nazi fleas on *them*!'

Every plane – Dakotas and Lancasters mostly – that flew out with supplies for the troops came back with a load of liberated prisoners. Then, with train passes in their pockets, they were sent home for forty-two days' leave.

So there they are – Abigail, Molly, Adam, Ivy and young William – waiting on the platform with a hundred other people on a breezy sunny morning in spring. The train steams in and slows to a stop, every compartment crammed with POWs; confused, cheerful, rowdy. Where the hell *are* we?

And there's a reception on the platform. Despite food rationing, there are cakes, drinks, cigarettes and tea. It's unbelievable! And a big bed-sheet with WELCOME HOME painted on it.

Windows are lowered, doors opened; some of the people on the platform get in to welcome the prisoners, some of the prisoners get out to sample the food. There's a row with the guard over the delay, and the driver gets more steamed up than his engine.

They are underweight and half-starved, these men, with weary grinning faces. They can hardly believe what's happening. They were all given new uniforms at their transit camp, but they're creased and they don't fit. They make their skinny bodies seem even smaller. Their caps are all wrong, and some are wearing the peaked caps of German officers. ('The guards just scarpered and left everything!' one of them explains.)

What a mix they are! There are a couple of Scots from the Camerons, Australians, New Zealanders, Canadians. There are three Sikhs and a couple of Poles; this isn't a homecoming for *them*. But, better than a Jerry POW camp!

Molly is serving tea and buns on the platform, helped by Adam. William is wandering among the POWs at leg-level, happily watchful. And Ivy is flirting with a group of Londoners, unshaven, thin-faced, cheered beyond all reason by the presence of a pretty young woman.

Two of their friends – Cassie Covington and her foster-brother Edward Barrett – are there too. A young lieutenant on the train falls instantly in love with Cassie and longs to get out of the train and tell her so. But he knows he mustn't. And anyway, the boy beside her – younger, and in school uniform – is watchful and on guard.

Abigail sees that there are young men looking lost and ill, unable to rejoice. She goes from one to the other, ministering to them, recognising the darkness she finds in them. She lights a cigarette for one man – he can't strike a match because he's only got one arm. 'Grenade blew up before I could throw it,' he says. 'Nothing heroic.' She sits beside him, lights up hesistantly, and transfers the cigarette from her lips to his.

Adam is shown a mouth organ, a trophy from a German prison guard. 'But will it play English tunes?' someone jokes.

'Let's see,' Adam says.

After a few experimental squawks, he begins to play, and everyone starts to sing, *There'll be bluebirds over The White Cliffs of Dover. . .*

'I didn't know you could play a mouth organ,' Molly

says to Adam as she pours more water into a tea urn.

The man with one arm doesn't join in the singing. 'Can I write to you?' he says to Abigail.

Abigail doesn't hesitate for a second. 'Yes,' she says, 'of course.' She scribbles her address on his cigarette packet and pushes it into the pocket of his tunic.

The Deeping policeman has arrived. He blows his whistle and shouts for quiet. 'These men are all going home today!' he shouts. (Loud cheers.) 'One poor blighter has to get all the way to Belfast! (Groans.) They'll miss their connections if we delay them any more.' (More cheers.)

Abigail's young man is anxious to tell her something. It's important. He clutches her collar with his one hand. 'The pilot who flew us back,' he says, 'made a detour over the cliffs of Dover.' He puts his head on her shoulder and begins to cry, as if his heart is breaking.

Abigail finds she knows what to do. She holds him, says meaningless things to help.

Then Great Deeping's greengrocer arrives on his bike, with a great basket of – no! it's unbelievable! – *oranges*! Precious oranges! He races onto the platform and people grab them and throw them into the open windows for the POWs to catch.

Ivy, unnoticed, slips an orange into the pocket of her skirt.

The guard blows his whistle, the engine gives a blast. The last of the men climb back on board, local people get off, and the train pulls out. Windows lowered, grinning faces, arms waving. *Thank you! Thank you! Good luck in civvy street! Goodbye! Cheerio! God bless!*

Abigail catches a glimpse of her young man, excluded, wet-cheeked, gazing into space.

19

Molly and Abigail were capable of becoming ten-year-olds in an instant if it suited them.

That happened one day after school when they were upstairs in Abigail's bedroom revising for a French test. They saw a man hesitating in the road at Abigail's garden gate. He was dressed in a dark pinstripe suit, with a bowler hat and a furled umbrella, and shiny brown shoes. Nobody in Great Deeping dressed like that.

There was nothing finicky about him, however. He opened the gate, strode purposefully along the garden path and knocked on the front door.

The two oversized ten-year-olds pulled aside the rug and stretched eagerly on the floor, each with an ear to the wooden boards. Completely without shame. Below them was the living room and sure enough they heard Mrs Murfitt inviting him to come in and take a seat.

'You are Mrs Murfitt? Private Michael Murfitt's wife?'

' – Good. I won't introduce myself, if you don't mind. I'm not officially here. But I can tell you that I am your husband's commanding officer.'

Abigail's hair – close to Molly's eyes – was like spun gold in the afternoon sun. She was a girl in a fairy-tale attic.

'Mrs Murfitt, when did you last hear from your husband?'

'Shortly before Dunkirk. In 1940.' Her voice was rough-edged.

'Did you think he was dead?'

'We had the usual message – he was missing, presumed killed.'

'And nothing since?'

The floorboards were warm and rough on Molly's cheek, smelling of dusty wood. Everything was ten times clearer to her vision that afternoon. This happened sometimes – lines became as sharp and cold as ice, colours were deep and luminous. Objects only inches away became as deep and fathomless as a translucent ocean. The silvery hairs on Abigail's arm belonged to a different and lustrous universe where everything was new and reborn every time you looked at it.

'I won't beat about the bush, Mrs Murfitt. I've come to tell you that he is alive and well. Not *very* well, but *quite* well.'

Molly – with the shock of a sudden focusing – realised that Abigail's eyes were staring into hers, tragically, from six inches away.

'Are you surprised?'

A tricky moment. Then Mrs Murfitt said, 'I don't know what I am!' Her voice was savage. It must have

107

surprised the visitor. It didn't surprise the two listeners because they knew that was Mrs Murfitt's way.

'When can I see him?'

'Ah! That is the main reason I've come to see you. I'm afraid you *can't* see him. And you *mustn't*. Not yet, anyway.'

Mrs Murfitt must have looked her question. He explained. 'During the German occupation of France, your husband was unofficially working for Secret Intelligence. But he hadn't been recruited by them and he hadn't been trained by them. He wasn't with his regiment, and he wasn't a POW. So – technically – he has to be regarded as *absent without leave.*'

Downstairs there was an outburst they couldn't hear properly. Then, 'We don't shoot deserters any more, Mrs Murfitt.'

A trapped fly buzzed at Abigail's bedroom window and Molly's enchanted vision of Abigail changed. She was no longer a young girl in a sunlit fairy-tale, but the tall fifteen-year-old girl she really was. Long and strong, with a grown-up distress. *Fear*, even.

'Let me explain. Private Murfitt is alive and in London. He has been given compassionate leave. But, until this matter is cleared up, he has been told to stay in London and not to contact you.'

A pause. 'I have no intention of allowing him to be charged with desertion. Believe me, *that won't happen.* But until I've cleared this up he is, technically, a prisoner on parole. He has had absolute orders – he must not leave London. And he must not contact his family.'

'It *will* be cleared up?'

'Yes. Absolutely! And there are other reasons why he cannot see you yet.'

A cloud passed over the sun and Abigail's bedroom was chilled. Abigail changed her position, crouching on the floorboards. But still listening. There were creases in her cheek.

'Your husband was not just a successful agent – he was a *very* successful one. So successful, in fact, that he became known to the Nazis. You know about the V-1 rockets?

'– Your husband located two of their main launching sites in France. He wasn't the only one, of course. There were others. Later, he located a V-2 launch-pad as well and allied bombers destroyed it. Saved hundreds of lives, probably.'

Another twist in the tangle. Now Abigail had to think of her father as a War hero.

'His name is known to the Gestapo. As far as the Germans are concerned, your husband is a wanted man.'

There was an agonised pause. Then Mrs Murfitt, almost inaudibly, said, 'But the Germans have been defeated.'

'Yes, of course. *Almost*. But, for a little while longer, we think it would be wise for him to stay under cover. They probably know where he lives.'

All three listeners took this in, fully and slowly.

'Besides,' the voice went on, 'we may need him in Germany.'

'Why? What could you possibly want him for now?'

'There's chaos in Germany, Mrs Murfitt. And in Poland and Czechoslovakia. Austria too. Millions of impoverished people. Factories obliterated by our bombing. No jobs, no money, no food. Refugees flooding in. There will be work for people with the skill and experience of your husband.'

'Work? How long for?' No sharpness now, just a husky weariness of the whole damn thing.

'A year, perhaps. But, Mrs Murfitt, the real reason I have come to see you is this. It is *very* important. Your husband has had a bad time. Almost five years behind enemy lines, in enemy-occupied territory! In constant danger. He is not quite himself now – and I'm afraid he might give way.'

'What do you mean, *give way*?'

'I mean that he might be tempted to come to see you. He must not do that. *And if he does, you must make him go back to London, at once.*'

Then Abigail understood. That man downstairs *knew* that her dad had already been home. He had come to warn them.

'I must go, Mrs Murfitt. The matter will be resolved in three or four weeks. I will see that it is. But for the time being this is the way it must be. Goodbye.'

Abigail had listened in silence long enough. Downstairs with her mum she let rip. 'Deserted!' she cried angrily. '*Deserted!* How dare they say he deserted? He's been a hero!'

But her mother didn't join in. She stood at the window, looking out towards the railway, leaning heavily on her arms, saying nothing.

Molly felt she should try to calm Abigail. 'The man didn't say your dad *was* a deserter. Just that it had to be cleared up.'

Mrs Murfitt turned round. 'Why couldn't your father have got himself killed five years ago?' she said. Her voice was shrill and fierce. It scared them. 'Like ordinary soldiers! Why couldn't he just have got himself *shot*? Or taken prisoner! But *no*! He has to be a hero without telling anyone!'

'*Mum!*' Abigail's headlong emotion was stopped in its tracks. In an uncertain voice she said: 'Mum, Dad's back. Aren't you glad?'

'Are *you*? Are *you* glad he's back?' Mrs Murfitt said. 'We buried him five years ago. In our heads, we buried him and grieved for him! And I *know* you grieved, I *know* how unhappy you were! And I grieved too – believe me, I *did*! It was *hard work*, doing that! All those years I was learning to be a widow. And then he comes *back*!'

Molly had a half-glimpsed understanding. How could they unravel that knitted-up grief?

'Except that he *hasn't* come back. Even that isn't

normal. He's come back, but he's supposed to stay away! And if they ever let him back properly, he's going away again!'

'Mum . . . ' No anger now, just fear and uncertainty.

'This War is ending – and d'you know what? There are two types of family. All over the country. There are the happy ones, overjoyed that their loved ones are coming home. What a time they have to look forward to! And there are the others – think of them, you two! When everyone else is having parties and carnivals to celebrate, there'll be some left alone, knowing *their* loved ones aren't ever coming back.'

Her voice had lost its energy now; her anger was wearing itself out.

'I thought I belonged to that group. But I don't. There's a third group, a special group for *me*! Your father has made sure of that.'

Molly forgot for a moment that this was not her own family. She ought to have said nothing, but she was such a believer in things as they should be that she couldn't help herself. 'But you belong to the first group,' she said. 'Your loved one *is* coming home.'

Mrs Murfitt looked at Molly, smiled weakly, and said, 'I must get on. The spuds won't peel themselves.'

20

Is it ever going to end? people said to each other as still the War dragged on.

Then one evening it was announced on the wireless that the War in Europe was over. The Prime Minister, Winston Churchill, would announce it officially at three o'clock the next day. At the same moment, similar announcements would be made in Washington and Moscow. Germany had been defeated.

The next day would be V.E. Day, Victory in Europe Day. The day after would be a holiday as well.

Peace at last!

Molly, Adam and Abigail were too excited to stay at home. Ivy was the same. They walked into town, expecting to find signs of jubilation. They heard some feeble singing in a pub, but apart from that there was nothing at all. *The church bells*, Molly thought – *surely they'd be ringing on such a day!*

'It's as if everyone's asleep,' Abigail said.

They felt moody and restless. 'I bet it's different in London,' Ivy grumbled.

'Let's go there then!'

'*What?*'

'Well, why not?'

'We might see the king!'

'Or Mr Churchill.'

'Let's go *tonight*!'

'What *now*?'

'They'll never let us.'

It was a crazy idea. What parent would allow them to spend the night in the streets of London?

'Ivy will be with us,' Molly said to her mum.

Ivy grimaced. 'Don't look at me! *I'm* not looking after them!'

'*And* Adam,' Molly said.

They persuaded their friends Cassie and Edward to go with them, and that made it all right. A group of six, their mothers thought, would surely be safe.

So, with bags of picnic food, bottles of drink, and some rugs, they travelled to Liverpool Street on the last train.

It was a tired and worn-out train, part of a tired and war-worn railway – ill-lit, smelling of cigarette smoke, and slow; and there was hardly anyone else on it. The world seemed to have crept away and gone to sleep. The guard didn't come for their tickets; he was probably asleep too.

Even the weather was wrong. The air was stuffy and oppressive. Liverpool Street station was cavernous and empty.

Adam led the way through the streets. It was the first time for more than five years that he had seen his city with the streetlights lit. Molly saw him stop, to take it all in.

Most Londoners had gone to bed and those who were left in the streets walked about silently, as if they were lost or looking for something. Everyone had had enough of this War – now it was over, they were too bloody tired to care!

The air was suffocating and the sky dense and overcast.

They found an all-night café and managed to pass away an hour there. But no one else came in and when she'd served them the waitress fell asleep behind the till. When they left, fat drops of rain fell on them, a short half-hearted blitz. 'There's going to be a storm,' someone said from a doorway. From inside the building someone answered, 'Better than one of Hitler's!' and there was laughter. 'You coming to bed, Tommy? I'm worn out!'

The rain stopped. Adam suddenly muttered, '*Run!*' and they followed him through streets and passageways illuminated by rapid lightning flashes. Then came a great crash of thunder from just above their heads, followed by a long incessant roar. Adam led them into a churchyard. There was no church, only a bombed-out ruin. But the doorway and porch were intact, with a roof.

They heard a hissing roar, a torrential downpour

approaching. It reached the church just as they scrambled into the porch, breathless and excited.

Picnic time, they decided. As they ate they were joined by other refugees from the storm. A gloomy airman, with kitbag and greatcoat. An old man with a shivering lurcher, who told them that him and his ole pal Whipper had been homeless since 1943. And a smart young woman in high-heeled shoes, who leaned against the doorway smoking non-stop with shaking fingers.

Tiredness overcame them eventually. They sat on the floor, their backs against the wall, pressing close, with one folded rug to sit on and the others covering their legs. Sleep was patchy and uncomfortable. Cassie fell asleep on Edward's shoulder, and Edward stayed awake, watchful and happy. Out in the darkness, the storm rumbled on and the rain came relentlessly down as if it would never stop.

Molly slept briefly, then awoke from a dream. She shifted to a less uncomfortable position and peered into the strange darkness. It was like a scene in a black-and-white film, where nobody talked. She shivered. This was no film – she was *in* it.

In the dream, she had shrugged off her naked skin, like a snake.

Adam awoke first, needing to pee.

He yawned, stretched, and went outside into the sunlight of a clear dawn, washed and fresh, with a

116

flawless sky, and the wet pavements drying. Edward followed and found him gazing up at St Paul's Cathedral, immense and enchanted in the dawn sunshine, almost undamaged despite five years of bombing.

From a tree somewhere in the blackened graveyard a blackbird began its dawn song. *Wake up, world! This is the best time of our lives!*

'I'm off!' Ivy announced.

Abigail protested. 'I'm going to meet someone,' Ivy said – as if they ought to have known all along that she'd no intention of spending the day with them.

'But who will look after us?' Adam said innocently.

Ivy just pulled one of her faces. 'I'll meet you at the station tonight – 9.30,' she said. 'And make sure you're there!' she added – as if, somehow, that covered her responsibility.

'Want to come for a drink, Frosty? Later?'

It was quiet that morning in Mercer's Lane market. Still, the place was waking up and there were a few people about. Two boy scouts were setting up a ladder to fix a string of bunting across the street.

A postman sped into the market-place on his bike, and a flock of startled pigeons took off and wheeled up to the rooftops. Their wings clattered and flashed in the sunlight. There was a long queue in the main road, waiting for a bus to the West End. They were right under the birds' flight path. An elderly woman grumbled, 'Would you Adam-and-Eve it? Look at the front of my best coat!' Of course, everyone laughed. 'It's supposed to mean good luck, Mavis,' someone said.

'No, thanks. I've got an appointment,' Frosty said.

Raised eyebrows, mocking and sarcastic. The Maggot's face said, *Who would want an appointment with you?* But his mouth said, 'About those shirts, Frosty.'

'What about them?'

'They're very good. First class quality, in fact.'

'Good enough, are they, for your posh clee-on-tell?'

'Trouble is, there ain't enough of 'em. I need them in hundreds, not dozens.'

'I can't get them in hundreds.'

'You could get rich, Frosty.' His voice was a smoker's growl.

'Well, I can't. It's risky. Anyway, it would be *you* getting rich. Not me.'

The older man shrugged his smartly padded shoulders. 'Naturally. But if you ain't prepared to take risks, you ain't never going to get nowhere. Especially in peacetime. People will pay good money for stuff that don't need no coupons, know what I mean?'

'I've got my eye on something else.'

'Oho! What sort of something else?'

'A different product. For a better clee-on-tell.'

The Maggot tilted his head sideways, disbelieving, mocking. He peered up, holding Frosty's eye with his usual interested look. Then he gently brushed a fleck of dirt from Frosty's coat collar. It made Frosty nervous. He looked away, at a passing soldier who had stopped to hold the bottom of the ladder while one of the scouts climbed up.

'Please yourself. If you change your mind, we'll be at the *Bull and Butcher*. Around dinnertime.'

'I'm meeting someone,' Frosty said.

The streets were becoming crowded. People were walking in the middle of the road, all heading west. Buses and taxis edged their way among them, brushing their bodies. Progress was slow, so Adam took them down a side street to the Embankment. But it was just as crowded there.

'We might see your dad,' Molly said to Adam.

It was unlikely, in this crowd.

'We might see mine,' Abigail said.

There was a group of people singing, sailors mostly, arm-in-arm with people in the crowd. They formed a semi-circle and surged backwards and forwards, singing 'Knees Up Mother Brown'. Then someone started up another popular wartime song, with its treacherous and irresistible words. 'We'll Meet Again', they all sang.

'Only we sodding-well *won't!*' a voice growled from close to them.

Not many people heard her – a middle-aged woman, arms folded, with her back against a wall. Some mad person, Molly thought. Embarrassed, she drew away, ashamed because she had no idea what to say. Adam saw a face, deep-eyed, dark-browed, heavily wrinkled, as if scoured and gouged by wind and weather.

Abigail 's vision was truer. She saw that the woman carried in her hand a small silver photo-frame with a picture of a young man. 'Is that your son?' she said.

The woman glared angrily at Abigail. 'He was nineteen.'

'He has your eyes.'

'Shot down over Cologne.'

While the other two waited, Abigail talked to the woman as if she'd known her all her life. Then something happened the wrong way round. Molly half-expected the grief-stricken mother to give way to tears (who could blame her?), and even perhaps that Abigail might comfort her. But it was suddenly Abigail who was crying, silently, with tears running down her face. And the woman put her arm around Abigail and held her, to quieten this unaccountable grief.

'Ridiculous!' Abigail said later. 'A total stranger!'

Mr Paterson Royce, art dealer to the rich, decided to shut his gallery and have a day off. I'll walk to Westminster, he thought. To see if anything's doing.

First, though, he decided to remove the criss-crossed sticky tape that had been on his gallery window since the start of the War. He was feeling pleased with himself.

In the last few days he'd sold the Picasso drawing, and all the Picasso prints. Two art collectors had come in and paid cash.

He put some replacement prints on display (*not* Picassos, alas), locked up, and joined the crowds moving towards Parliament Square.

London was waking up to a new dawn. To peace. And hopefully, Mr Royce thought, a flourishing art market.

Crowds everywhere!

People having breakfast outside Buckingham Palace. Early-comers settling close to the barbed wire in Parliament Square. Dealers selling flags, red-white-and-blue hair-ribbons, paper hats, victory rosettes. Union jacks all over the place.

Crowds in Whitehall, in Parliament Street, in Parliament Square. Buses edging slowly through, small children riding on grown-ups' shoulders, people on bikes. And loftily high above everyone else the mounted police. Cars with people on their roofs and bonnets, young servicemen sitting astride the tops of lamp-posts. A crowd of riotous land-army girls. People on balconies, cheering, waving, calling to people they knew down in the street.

Where had all these carnival-people come from? Last night the place had been more dead than alive!

Girls kept getting kissed. A couple of times young

men tried it on with Cassie, but she put on her haughty touch-me-not look and they drew back. But Molly and Abigail were kissed several times, and learned to enjoy it as part of their tribute. Some sailors heaved one girl onto the roof of a single-decker bus. But the bus jerked into movement and she staggered and fell back into the crowd, where she was caught in a tangle of friendly arms, emerging unhurt and happy. She blushed, grinned, straightened her skirt and everyone cheered. More kissing.

Young men in uniform were leaning over a balcony, waving their hats, cheering and laughing. Adam saw a young officer drop his peaked cap over the edge.

There was an expression of mild surprise on Molly's face as the hat fell at her feet; and then a succession of unspoken meanings – amusement at what had happened, curiosity as she looked up, good-humoured helpfulness as she prepared to throw the hat back to the young officer, frowning determination as she took aim, laughing pride as she threw it accurately, then a cheerful acknowledgement of his *thank you!*

And not a word said.

Adam saw Molly glance back with a fleeting look of interest and affection. The young lieutenant was still watching her. All day Adam studied Molly. Expressions flowed across her face as fast as a stream in the mountains. How could he draw such *movement*? – the quick liftings and lowerings of her head, the meanings in her eyes, her thousand different ways of smiling.

They saw Mr Churchill arriving at Westminster, almost overwhelmed by cheering crowds. He walked the last few yards, with a car following. Molly was in an ecstasy to be so close to her hero.

There was a rumour that Princess Elizabeth and Princess Margaret were there, in the crowd. Molly and Abigail caught a glimpse of two nice-looking girls of about their own age who might have been the two princesses. They were too far away for certainty, but someone in that direction shouted *Three cheers for the Princesses!*

Young Edward felt uneasy in cities and he disliked crowds. Molly saw Cassie say something close and private into his ear. He looked gratefully at her and brightened up.

By the afternoon they were exhausted with heat and standing. In Trafalgar Square and Parliament Square tens of thousands of people stood in silence, listening intently as the King's speech was relayed by loudspeaker. All the usual sounds were stilled, as if the great city itself were paying attention to this quietly-spoken man.

When Mr Churchill made his broadcast to the nation, they forgot their tiredness and listened intently to the loudspeakers. He paid tribute to the men and women who had laid down their lives for victory, and to all those who had fought valiantly on land, sea and in the air. 'We may allow ourselves a brief period of rejoicing,' he said, 'but . . . we must now devote all our strength and resources to the completion of our task, both at home and abroad. *Advance Britannia!'*

There was a great roar of cheering from the crowd and a bellowing round of *For he's a jolly good fellow!* When the singers on the west side of the Square had finished, the singers on the east side had only just got to *And so say all of us!* Everyone on the west side laughed and everyone on the east side looked puzzled, wondering why.

The day wore on, sunny, warm and joyous. Outside Buckingham Palace, pressed and almost suffocated by the crowds, many dressed in red-white-and-blue, they cheered as the King and Queen and the two Princesses came out on to the balcony. Mr Churchill in his siren suit came out and conducted 'Land of Hope and Glory'. Everyone cheered and cheered, some people were crying, many were laughing.

But where were the people whose sons and husbands and lovers would never come home, Molly wondered. Sitting alone in quiet rooms, looking at old photographs perhaps, wondering how to get through the rest of their lives?

Much later, on their way back to the station, they saw weary revellers collapsing everywhere, resting. Many planned to spend the night there. Anywhere would do – on lawns in the park, on benches, in the porches of offices and hotels. On the steps of one of the most famous banks in the world an entire family was camping – granny and granddad, mum, auntie Gladys, several children, next-door neighbours, rugs, a child's potty and a wind-up gramophone with records.

Long after they had left, thousands of people converged on London's great monuments, which were floodlit specially. There were fireworks and effigies of Hitler burned on bonfires. In Piccadilly Circus a party was starting. There was dancing and the buses couldn't get through.

Adam's dad and all his staff stood by with nothing to do. 'Would you Adam-and-Eve it?' Bob Swales said. 'You'd think they'd had enough of fires and explosions!'

'I've never been as tired as this, in my whole life,' Molly said. They hardly had the energy to put one foot before the other as they drew near to Liverpool Street Station. They were exhausted, thirsty, and sweaty. Their heads ached, their legs ached, their throats were sore, their feet were swollen. For the last hour Cassie had walked barefoot, Edward carrying her shoes.

Inside the station they found Ivy, waiting. They had forgotten about her. And, even more surprising, Mr Whymper was there too, making it perfectly clear that he didn't want to travel back with them.

'He looks as if he's been up to something,' Molly said.

Abigail thought Mr Whymper was the most boring man in the world. 'He always looks like that – but he never *has* done anything!'

The train was at the platform, almost empty. They were able to occupy three whole compartments, Adam and Ivy in one, Abigail and Molly in the second, Cassie and Edward in the third. Wearily they took off their shoes, rubbed their aching legs, and stretched out, each on one of the long seats.

As the train steamed slowly through the East End, Molly reached across the compartment and touched Abigail. 'Let's be best friends for ever. Shall we?'

A sleepy reply. 'No.'

Molly lifted her head, startled. 'Why not?'

'I disapprove of your character. You're a flirt, Molly Barnes.'

'I am *not*!'

'You kissed half the men in London today.'

Molly yawned, slowly and thoughtfully. 'What about that captain in the Marines?'

'He needed mothering,' Abigail said.

'He was *old*! Thirty at least!'

Later, as the train was pulling out of Tottenham Hale, Abigail said, 'All right then. Yes, let's.'

Too late. Molly was asleep.

When they reached Great Deeping it was dark, the air fresh and cool.

They found that the town had at last woken up to the fact that the War was over. People stood in the streets, chatting in groups and laughing. Doors were open to let in the cool of the evening. Strings of bunting had been nailed from house to house across the streets. Flags had been fixed to drain-pipes and jammed into windows.

The next day there was to be a street party – the biggest party the town had ever had. People would set out their tables and chairs all along the Main Street and the High Street – a mile-long party! They would have to provide their own food and drink, of course. But there would be music and dancing. No one would go to bed until after midnight. And the smallest children would be allowed to stay up late.

That's what happened. The next day there was a grand Victory Parade through the town, led by the brass band. Then, in turn came: the Home Guard, local army Cadets, old soldiers from the Great War, with their medals, the Firemen, the ARP, the Land Army, the two district nurses, the Boys' Brigade, Scouts, Guides, Brownies, and Cubs, all in their best uniforms.

There were *two* brass bands, not just one – the town's silver band united with the Salvation Army band. The noise was terrific! *Two* big bass drums; *two* of everything (except that there was only one euphonium because Edward played in both bands). The parade was led by old George Watson, ex-sergeant-major from World War One, square and upright in his best dark suit and bowler hat, with his medals pinned on and his cane under his arm, as he'd done on every Armistice Sunday since 1919.

Molly is having a break in a large tranquil room on the fourth floor, with quiet walls, white wooden flooring, and a window reaching from end to end and from floor to ceiling. Her chair – made of pale-blue glass and shaped like a soup-ladle – is surprisingly restful.

Her granddaughter is kneeling on cushions with some sandwiches, reading *Peter Duck* by Arthur Ransome.

The street below is crowded with shoppers, policemen, taxis, and buses. No sound penetrates the triple-glazed window. A red bendy-bus silently stops below her. A number 73, she observes, as it pulls away.

An old wartime memory surfaces unexpectedly – a red double-decker. It was a number 73, and someone was waving a helpless hand from an upstairs window.

Her granddaughter puts down her book. For most of the time Carrie goes about her life preoccupied with her own thoughts. But from time to time she looks out and asks a penetrating question.

'Granny, are you unhappy because Granddad isn't here?'

A straight question deserves a straight answer, eye to eye, old person to young person.

'Yes.'

The interviewer joins them and they chat, informally. 'You went to Cambridge, I believe,' she says.

'Yes,' Molly says. Then she adds, 'No one in my family had ever been to university.'

'Why Cambridge?'

Molly smiles. 'The deputy head at my school believed we were all geniuses,' she says. 'She arranged trips for girls in the upper school – to open days at colleges. That sort of thing.'

She remembers it vividly – a dazzling afternoon in early summer, billowy and green and bright.

21

On a warm sunny Saturday in early June there was an Open Day at one of the colleges in Cambridge. A group of high school girls gaggled nervously around the porter's lodge and were admitted. They were mostly sixth-formers, a few girls from the fifth.

And Molly. *I shouldn't be here – I'm too young,* she thought.

It was a billowy afternoon, green and bright. Into the sunlight they moved, awed a little by the cloistered buildings, the forbidden lawn, and the tender long-flowered wisteria covering the walls. There were groups of students from other schools, mostly boys in bright blazers.

Now I'm here, what am I supposed to *do*? Molly wondered. She thought longingly of Ivy and Abigail, who were looking around the shops. That's what Great Deeping people did when they went to Cambridge – they went shopping.

There were stooped and stately men walking about, their black gowns grandly sweeping the grass. They all looked old – the young ones, Molly supposed, were in the War. She became separated from the girls from her own school and found herself by accident among a group of boys. They were tall, confident, talking in loud voices about scholarships. They ignored Molly. Hamish was probably here somewhere, but she hadn't seen him.

A woman in a gown was bearing down upon her and Molly tried to slip to the back of the group. She didn't want to be singled out.

But there was no escape. 'You look rather lost.'

She was tall, rather daunting. But her voice was kind, at odds with her appearance. 'I'm Professor Beale.'

'I thought all the professors were men,' Molly said. She was nervous. She wouldn't normally have said anything so abrupt.

'They are. But I'm not.' Professor Beale smiled, a huge toothy smile that curled around her face. 'We're supposed to talk about your higher education.'

'My *what*?'

'Coming to university,' the professor explained.

'I don't think I should have come at all,' Molly said in a burst of embarrassment. 'I'm too young!'

'How old are you?'

'Fifteen. Sixteen next month.'

'Well! It *is* a bit early. Never mind! What do you want to read?'

What a strange question! How could Molly begin to answer it? The list of books she wanted to read was endless.

But she was saved from embarrassment. 'English? History? One of the sciences?'

131

Then Molly understood. 'History,' she said eagerly. 'Well, *archaeology* really.' Her voice was breathy, but she didn't know how to stop it. I sound like a nervous schoolgirl, she thought crossly. Then, I *am* a nervous schoolgirl.

There was a pause. The savage eyes were glaring at her, mistrustfully. 'Where do you live? And, by the way, what is your name?'

'Molly Barnes,' Molly said. 'And I live in Great Deeping.'

'And where is that, pray, Miss Barnes?'

Molly had never been called *Miss Barnes* before. 'It's a town in the Fens,' she said.

'Let us sit,' said Professor Beale. She led Molly to a stone seat, and then continued. 'Aren't they magnificent? They're 220 years old.'

'*Who* are?' Molly was losing her grip on reality.

'The wisterias,' the Professor said. 'Do you believe in Fate?' she continued. 'You see, I am an archaeologist – the only one here today. It's rather strange that we should have singled each other out.'

Molly was utterly confused. Wisterias? Fate? What was she *on* about?

But the professor swept on. 'Miss Barnes,' she said, 'you live in the middle of the Fens. Correct?'

Molly nodded.

'To an archaeologist, the Fens have very little interest. There is hardly anything there! So please explain how a young woman living there can develop an interest in archaeology. It is one of the few places in the northern hemisphere where there *isn't* any archaeology!'

Molly protested. 'But there have been Roman treasures. And Viking hoards.'

That was when the Professor realised this girl was serious. 'Yes,' she said in a gentler voice, 'but they've been found in the foothills *around* the Fens, not *in* the Fens. It's a most unlikely part of the world to produce a young person with an interest in archaeology.'

Molly was on the edge of tears. *'But I've found a Roman road!'*

'Miss Barnes,' the Professor said firmly, 'it is *very* unlikely that you have found a Roman road in the Fens. During the Roman occupation the area was mostly under water.'

'I *know*!' Molly wailed. 'That's the *point*.'

Now it was Professor Beale who was confused. She tilted her head sideways, raised her brows questioningly, and waited for Molly to explain.

'It can't be a Roman road, so it has to be a *Norman* road! But whoever heard of a Norman road?'

'Describe it.'

Molly tried. A short length of solid road, made of rough square-cut stone. Sloping slightly.

'How did you find it?'

Molly breathed more calmly. 'It's near a pill-box.'

Did the Professor know what a pill-box was? In case she didn't, Molly added, 'One of the emplacements they built all over eastern England at the start of the

War. When the builder started to dig, he uncovered a few of these stones. Well, we saw them . . .'

'We?'

Molly was getting into her stride. 'I was with some friends. We go swimming there. I saw the stones beside the pill-box and thought they were interesting. So I took a spade and a brush and started uncovering some more.'

'You were swimming, did you say?'

'There is a mere – a big pond – and we swim there. It will be lovely when the weather's warmer. More than a pond really, almost a lake.'

There were more questions, and Molly described her Norman road, built of stones, and leading down into the water.

'Miss Barnes, will you show me your site?'

Sight? What was she talking about? Molly looked blank, showed her confusion, and waited.

'Your Norman road. I would like to see it. May I?'

Molly was profoundly flattered. A Cambridge Professor wanting to see her discovery! 'Oh,' she said doubtfully. And then, more loudly, '*Oh!*' as she suddenly – and a minute too late – understood about *site*. Then she said, 'I'd *love* you to come and see it.'

They had discovered the mere a few years ago.

On a bright warm morning they'd gone exploring. Behind their barn, a grassy track led to a small wooded

134

hill. Hardly a hill at all, really. But in the Fens, even the smallest rise in the ground would have been entirely surrounded by water in the old days.

They'd assumed it was just scrubland, of no interest to anyone. But when they reached the hill, they found a magical and totally surprising place, with an overgrown footpath leading through the trees – as if it had been waiting for them.

New young cow-parsley was everywhere, and tall grasses hardly moving in the warm still morning, with a bright spicing of buttercups. The trees were small, mostly hawthorn with leaf-buds bursting. There was a strong green smell, sharp and sweet, full of the coming summer.

Nobody ever came there, you could tell. It was a secret place.

It was a very small wood, and they quickly came to the other side of the hill – where, to their surprise, they found a military pill-box, squat and ugly, made of raw concrete, facing across the flat fenland fields. All around it the grass was shorter, almost a lawn, sloping gently down to the edge of a mere.

The water was black and clear and deep, entirely enclosed by sedges. A moorhen paddled her busy way across the surface, disappearing into the reeds. Four tiny moorchicks hurried after her. There was a willow-trunk, fallen headlong, lying just along the surface of the water – perfect for sitting on if you wanted to dabble your feet.

The pill-box was too small and too hard-edged to make a den of any kind – and anyway they had a den already, in their barn. But we could leave our swimming things here, they said. And the flat concrete roof was warm in the sunshine, ideal for sunbathing after a swim.

It was full of promise, this lovely place. And entirely secluded. Behind was the wood; in front the mere and its enclosing sedges. Then miles and miles of flat fields. In the distance, perhaps five miles away, they could see Littleport church humped among its trees. And a few hazy miles beyond that, Ely Cathedral.

No one ever came here and no one would know where they were. It was irresistible.

Later, they found out that the place had a name and was shown on maps. It was called Deepney Hill, and the pond was Deepney Mere.

It was here that Molly found her Norman road. A few stones were already exposed. She lifted the turf cleanly away, and found there were more.

It was a decisive moment. She was not seized by a sudden certainty, and there was no miraculous vision of her future life. But she found a new curiosity, patient and persistent. And focused. *This is where our history is,* she thought. *It's in the ground, underneath us!*

They took instant possession and it became their summer place. They sunbathed, they did their homework, they talked about Life. Adam worked on his drawings, Abigail read and Molly uncovered more of the Norman road.

And they swam. How they swam! Heedless of the cold, they plunged and wallowed in the silky water. Then, shivering and goosepimply, they would scramble out, clutching their shoulders for warmth and scurrying to the pill-box. Wrapped in towels with their feet pulled up under them, they would grow warm in the sun.

It was place of promise. And secrets.

No one ever found them there.

22

Ivy rushed into the house one bright evening in a state of agitation. Abigail's mum, tying up canes for her runner beans, glanced up but carried on with her work. Molly, Abigail and Adam sat at the kitchen table, doing homework. They too looked up. *Now* what? their faces said.

'Have you heard? The *Lurker* – he's back!' Ivy plonked herself onto a chair at the table.

'The Lurker?'

'*Yes!* He's been *seen*. Here – close to this house!'

Adam knew why Abigail and Molly shared puzzled glances at this news. He'd been told – but why was Ivy so disturbed by it?

'Who's seen him?'

'Lots of people – in the last few days.' Ivy lowered her voice to a frightened whisper. 'And it's always near here, by the railway!'

She looked from face to face, wide-eyed – like a frightened heroine in a silent movie, Adam thought.

'Calm down, Ivy,' Abigail said sharply. 'It won't be you he's interested in.'

'You don't know,' Ivy said. 'It might be.'

She went on in this vein for some time, hinting at something while Abigail scoffed. Then Ivy shoved her chair violently back and said, 'I've had enough of this! Come upstairs!'

In the bedroom, Ivy undid the top button of her blouse with impatient fingers and pulled out a chain. She ducked and pulled the chain over her head. It was threaded through a plain gold ring.

She held it in front of them on the palm of her hand. All four heads leaned close.

'It's a wedding ring,' Molly said cautiously.

Abigail knew about the ring; she'd seen it when Ivy got undressed at night.

'Is it your mum's?' Adam said.

'My mum never *had* a wedding ring!' Ivy snapped. 'And they never found her rings anyway. Nor her fingers, come to that.'

The brutality of this shook all four of them. Ivy was aghast that she'd said it, the others shocked by the fact of it.

'Whose is it then?'

Ivy's voice was defiant. 'It's mine!'

'*Yours?*'

Interesting, thought Adam.

'I don't believe you!' Abigail said.

Ivy got to her feet and rummaged in one of the drawers of the dressing-table. She took out a stiff brown envelope, and from that she pulled a photograph.

They looked at it, slowly taking it in: Ivy, smiling

shyly, with a bouquet of roses in one hand and the other tucked in the arm of a handsome young soldier. The ring was clearly visible.

'We got married last summer, in June. You can see the certificate, if you want. His name's Murray.'

'*Married?*'

'*Murray?*'

'Yes. Murray Lea.'

In a fake American accent Adam said, 'So it's bye bye Miss Westgate, and hello Mrs Lea!'

Ivy told her story. Their disbelief faded as they slowly got used to this new state of affairs. She'd met him at a dance when he was on leave. In West London. 'He was doing the jitterbug when I first saw him,' she said. 'Lor, he couldn't half jive! We got on ever so well.'

Ivy thought back. 'When he went back to his base, he wrote to me. Then after about a month he said he was being posted abroad, and would I marry him?'

'And you said yes?' Molly was incredulous.

'Yes, I did,' Ivy said defiantly. 'Why shouldn't I? Anyway, he got ten days' embarkation leave and we went up to Carlisle where his family lived. While we were there, we went to Scotland and got married.'

'But you weren't old enough.'

'I *was*! You only have to be sixteen in Scotland, so *there*! And you don't need permission from your parents either!'

'I thought you had to live there for a few weeks,' Abigail said. She was profoundly suspicious.

'You're supposed to – but they made an exception because he was being posted abroad.'

'Were you in love with him?' Molly asked.

Ivy pulled one of her faces. 'I dunno,' she said.

'Did you have a honeymoon?'

''Course we did! Two nights and three days. Then I went to Liverpool with him, to his ship. He went to Burma and I went back home.'

'And you haven't seen him since?'

Ivy shook her head. 'The Lurker might be him,' she said.

'You think he's just popped back from Burma to see you?' Adam said.

Ivy turned on Adam. 'It's all very well for you to be sarky, Adam Swales,' she said savagely. 'Everyone knows you don't have any feelings! All you ever do is work out if you want to put people in your ruddy pictures!'

Adam raised an untroubled and ironic eyebrow at her.

Molly registered this criticism of Adam. She would think about it later. 'Were you happy?' she asked.

'It was all right,' Ivy said. 'But then he went – and I haven't seen him since.'

They absorbed this.

'Has he written?'

Ivy shook her head.

'Well, he'll be back soon.'

There was a pause then. None of them could quite

manage to refigure Ivy as a wife. It seemed impossible.

Something remained unsaid. Then Ivy said it. 'I don't want him to come back.'

'You won't have any choice!'

'Is that why you kept it a secret?'

Ivy nodded miserably.

'But he's your husband – he's *bound* to come back.'

Ivy stared down at her wedding photo. 'Was he unkind to you?' Molly said.

Ivy shook her head. 'He was OK. It's just that I can't remember . . . *I don't know anything about him at all!*' She stared at them in disbelief. 'I can't even remember what colour eyes he had! And now I'm stuck with him for the rest of my life!'

Molly imagined such a homecoming: two married strangers, the closeness, the embarrassment.

'Why should you think your husband is the Lurker?' Abigail demanded. 'You said he was posted to Burma.'

'He might not have gone. He might have deserted.'

Such things did happen, they knew. 'Army wives get some of their husbands' pay, don't they?'

Poor Ivy's face was bleak. 'Well, I've never had any.'

Adam had been silent through most of this. But a question occurred to him. 'On V.E. Day, when we all went to London, where did you go?'

Ivy flared up again. 'That's none of your business, Adam Swales! I've got friends, just like anybody else. And another thing – I don't want anyone knowing that I'm married! *No one!* And especially not your mum,

142

Abigail Murfitt! So you keep your mouths shut. I wish I'd never told you!'

In her vegetable garden, Mrs Murfitt tied the last of the canes and took the string and scissors back to the shed. As she turned to leave, she noticed a piece of paper, folded and pinned to the inside of the door. A message had been pencilled on it: *The enquiry is on Monday. Soon I'll be able to come home.*

She leaned her arms on the bench and stared, unseeing, out of the grimy shed window.

'She's full of surprises, our Ivy!' Adam said later.

'It's not surprises that she's full of,' Abigail said. 'It's *secrets*! All these months and she's never said a word!'

'We keep secrets from her,' Molly said.

'No we don't!'

'We've never told her about the mere.'

'She'd hate it there,' Abigail said. 'That's *our* place.'

There was a short silence as each of them acknowledged this shared private meanness. It was clear to all of them that Ivy would *hate* the mere.

23

One evening Mr Elmore Whymper – always quiet, always attentive to everything that was going on around him – took them by surprise. 'I have to go to Norwich tomorrow,' he said. 'There's a man I know there who's an expert on modern art. I wondered if Adam would let me take one of his drawings – just to show him.'

They were all in the kitchen. Supper was over, and there was a scatter of drawings on the table.

Adam was surprised, certainly. But he didn't object. 'Yes,' he said. 'Help yourself.'

So Mr Whymper chose one of the Picasso-style drawings and put it with elaborate care inside a large envelope. 'Thank you,' he said.

Adam's art teacher wanted to show some of his work to Mr Paterson Royce, the London art dealer. So one warm and sunny Saturday, Adam planned to spend the day at the mere arranging his artwork in a folder.

He became aware that little William was standing beside him, looking up.

'Want to come?'

William nodded happily.

William had a model yacht, about eighteen inches long, carved out of solid wood, with sails and rigging. It was bright red with white sails and Adam had painted its name on the stern, *Saucy Sue*. William planned to sail it on the mere.

At the pill-box, Adam settled down with a drawing-board and a disorderly bundle of drawings. William took off all his clothes and planned his boat's first voyage.

With its rigging loose and free, the *Saucy Sue* sailed a straight and elegant course in even the gentlest breeze. So William carried the boat right round to the distant edge of the mere. Adam saw him on the far side of the water, pushing through the reeds down to the water's edge. Then he crouched, launched the *Saucy Sue*, and straightened up to watch her as she set off on her perilous voyage across the wide Pacific.

Then he raced back to where Adam was, and watched as the boat gently nudged her way into harbour.

Adam made a quick affectionate sketch of William, standing at the water's edge. They shared a precious bar of chocolate.

Later, however, there was a disaster at sea. Out in the deepest part of the mere there was a clump of rotted reeds, all that was left of a coot's nest from the previous summer. The *Saucy Sue* had sailed into it and was firmly stuck.

'An uncharted island,' Adam said.

William nodded gravely.

Adam stripped and waded down into the water, leaning forward to swim out to sea.

William stood on the edge of the mere and watched as Adam reached the coot's nest and freed the *Saucy Sue*. Then he set it sailing again, back towards William. He trod water to watch, his streaming head and shoulders as big as the boat, like Neptune rising from the depths of the ocean.

Then he struck out for the shore.

In town, with her shopping completed, Molly had a shock. She saw Professor Beale coming out of the churchyard. She'd seen Molly and was making a beeline for her.

'Miss Barnes!' she cried. 'How timely!'

Molly, sounding unintentionally rude, said, 'What are *you* doing here?' Abigail nudged Molly at the *Miss Barnes* and Molly nudged Abigail to shut up.

'I found out your address,' she said. 'I've come to see your Norman road.'

Molly remembered her manners and introduced the Professor to Abigail, who said how-d'you-do as if she met professors every day of her life.

Escorting the Professor along the High Street, Molly felt a mixture of pride and embarrassment. Pride because Professor Beale was an interesting person to be seen with, in her long dark-red skirt, high-necked blue blouse, and a head-scarf that matched the skirt. But embarrassment too – because she carried an enormous hamper strapped on her back.

The shopping had to be taken home first; then Molly's mum (hastily whipping off her apron) had to be introduced; and their picnic lunches had to be packed. But at last they set off to Deepney Mere.

And that is how it happened that Professor Beale and Molly and Abigail walked out of the trees just as Adam walked out of the water, naked and streaming.

Abigail bit her lower lip and covered her mouth with her fists to keep in the snorts of laughter threatening to burst out. Molly was almost overwhelmed with embarrassment – she felt sure the professor had never seen male nakedness. *Two* naked males. Little William, muddy and also bare, stared at the newcomer.

'Oh!' Adam said. There was a towel in the pill-box and he walked up the grassy slope to get it.

Hurry up*!* Molly thought to herself in agony. *Get* on *with it!* But Adam was in no hurry. He paused at the water's edge to sleek his wet hair back from his face.

'Another of your friends?' Professor Beale said, turning to Molly. There seemed to be no sarcasm in her words, no amusement, no embarrassment. And certainly none of the disapproval they might have expected.

'Yes,' Abigail said, grinning widely. 'That's Adam.' (All of him! she thought wickedly.) 'And this is Molly's brother, William.' Molly herself was too tense to speak.

William looked anxiously at the newcomer's face. Strangers were inclined to ask questions and expect him to answer. But Professor Beale just said quietly that she was pleased to meet him, and left it at that.

They shared picnics.

Professor Beale brought from her enormous basket a small stool, a tiny collapsible table, a picnic-box and a thermos flask. She offered her four companions a pork pie – she disliked pork pies, she said – and two pasties – made mostly of potato and saw-dust, according to her.

These gifts were greedily accepted. Abigail asked what she would like to have from their picnic, in exchange. 'Hard-boiled eggs!' Professor Beale cried. 'What joy!'

'Fresh this morning,' Abigail said. 'I collected them myself.'

The professor treated Abigail to one of her huge curly smiles. 'What arrangements have you made for latrines?' she asked.

There was a short agonised silence while they worked out what she was talking about. 'Over there,' Adam said. 'Behind that hawthorn. We've dug a hole. Do you need to use it?'

Professor Beale shook her head. 'Just curious to know how you manage. It's the first requirement of a good camp.'

'It's never mentioned in camping stories,' Abigail said.

'I know. I once rebuked Arthur Ransome on that very point! Your Swallows and Amazons, I said . . . '

'You *know* Arthur Ransome?' Molly couldn't believe her ears. That was much more impressive than being a professor at Cambridge.

'I first met him in the Baltic. I was on a dig. That was before he wrote *Swallows and Amazons*, of course.'

Later, Professor Beale admired Adam's drawings. *Genuinely* admired them, apparently. Molly half-expected her to say that Picasso too was an old friend of hers.

When the meal was over and there could be no further reasons for delay, Molly said shyly, 'Would you like to see the Norman road now?'

Everyone paid attention as the Professor stared for a moment or two at the squared stone-work that Molly had uncovered. She paced about, and asked a few questions. 'How far does it extend?'

'I don't know how far it goes back into the wood. I'd have to clear away more of the earth – and I think I need the owner's permission before I do that.'

'Quite right. And the other end?'

'It goes into the water and then stops. After about three yards.'

'Is the end squared off?'

'Yes.'

'It's not a Norman road,' Professor Beale said eventually. 'It's later than Norman.'

They stood gloomily, waiting for Molly's inevitable disappointment.

'But it *is* mediaeval. I think it's a mediaeval jetty. Fifteenth century, I would guess. Perhaps late fourteenth.'

'A *jetty*?'

'Yes. For tying up boats and unloading them.'

They knew what a jetty was, but this seemed such an unlikely place for one.

'You see, it's built of the same kind of stone as your church,' Professor Beale said. 'There is no stone quarry anywhere near Great Deeping. So the stone for your church would have been brought here. And there wouldn't have been any good roads. Only water.'

Molly began to see it in her mind's eye. 'By boat?' she said.

'Precisely! By boat. Barge, probably. And when the stone began to arrive, they used some of it to build a jetty.'

'As you know, a good archaeologist writes a report,' the professor said to Molly later. 'You must describe what you've found, and how you found it. With maps and pictures. Then you add any local history which may have a bearing on it. Then you conclude with your suggested interpretation.'

'The jetty?'

'Yes. But that's *my* interpretation. You may suggest that, but you will as a matter of course acknowledge me.'

Molly looked flustered.

'Something like *Professor Anastasia Beale of St Adelaide's College, Cambridge, has suggested that . . .*'

'Oh, I *see!*'

'And when I refer to this discovery (which I certainly *shall*), I shall of course acknowledge *you*.'

'Oh!' Molly said happily.

'When you apply to university, I do hope you'll apply to my College.'

Molly looked troubled. 'I don't think my parents will let me go to university at all,' she said.

Professor Beale was thoughtful, and for one foolish hopeful moment Molly wondered if she might speak to her father and explain to him that his daughter was clearly a genius. And how wrong it would be to stand in her way.

But no. 'That's a battle you must fight for yourself,' Professor Beale said.

But when her basket was packed and she was ready to go, she paused. 'We are entering a new world,' she said. 'There have been two of the worst wars in history. If the human race is to put that in the past, we will need all the intelligent and well-educated women we can find!'

Before she left, Professor Beale bent down in front of

William to say goodbye. 'You've got goose-pimples all over,' she said gently. 'Don't you think you should put your clothes on?'

William nodded gravely, and Professor Beale stood up, said an airy thank you to all of them, hoisted her basket onto her shoulders, and set off into the trees.

24

All through the War Molly had felt safe most of the time. Now that peace had come, there were dangers and uncertainties on every side. The brightness of the sun seemed dark, people's faces were hard-edged and dangerous, the air crackled. People were unfamiliar, and unpredictable.

She walked on shifting sands that month, in a season of craziness. And there was to be a general election.

Mr Whymper was part of the strangeness. He cleared his throat shyly one day and said. 'Adam, I showed my friend your drawing.'

'Did he like it?'

'He offered me £15 for it,' Mr Whymper announced. 'Cash down! On the spot.'

It was an enormous amount of money! But Adam seemed unmoved. 'You should have taken it,' he said.

On the afternoon of election day everyone was sitting in the back garden. Mr Barnes had been on duty at one of the polling stations and had come home for some tea; Mr Whymper had just arrived back from Norwich.

'Oh, but I couldn't!' Mr Whymper said. 'It wasn't mine to sell. I would never . . . ' His long fingers fidgeted and fluttered nervously as he took the drawing from its envelope. He handed it back to Adam as if it were too hot to handle.

'Adam,' Mrs Barnes said, 'I've had a letter . . . '

(*Is this the end?* Molly thought to herself.)

'From my dad?'

'No. It's an official letter from London – about evacuees. It says there'll be no more money for your accommodation. They will pay until the end of term. But after that . . . '

(*But that's only two more weeks!*)

'I'd better start packing then,' Adam said.

Molly felt as if her skin were twice as sensitive as it should be. Everything that happened was bruising and hurtful. (*Is that all he can say?*)

'Most of the other evacuees have already gone back,' Mr Barnes pointed out.

(*I hate my dad! Why did he have to say that?*)

'Adam, listen. We've talked it over and we'd like you to stay here until the end of the summer holidays. If you'd like to. As our guest, I mean. But, well . . . in September I'm afraid there's nothing for it. Because you'll have to start at your new school in London.'

(*What can I do to stop this?*)

'Has your father said anything about it?'

But letters from Adam's parents had made no mention of it.

'If it were up to me, Adam,' Mrs Barnes said, 'you could stay here *always*.' She went round to him and hugged him from behind so that he almost fell backwards off his stool. (*She's always doing that!*) 'I'm going to miss you terribly!'

Mr Barnes pursed his lips. He and Molly exchanged a brief glance. William climbed on to Molly's lap and snuggled there unhappily.

There was a sudden squeal of bicycle brakes and Hamish Macaulay came speeding through the garden gate, swung his leg elegantly over the saddle, and dismounted in style.

Abigail was all mischief that day. 'Oh, look! Hamish has come to discuss the election with you,' she said quietly to Molly.

Molly seized up.

There were eager cheerful greetings, especially from Mr Barnes. And eager cheerful excitement when Hamish announced that he'd cycled to the strawberry fields near Wisbech and filled four big punnets. Enough for a feast!

They had no cream, what with rationing. And only enough sugar for a light sprinkling. Still, a feast it was.

Something in Hamish brought Molly's dad to life. He became animated and talkative, and they exchanged eager ideas about the election.

'My sister believes . . . '

(*He has a sister?*)

'. . . there will be a worldwide Labour movement.'

Mr Barnes smiled and asked how old his sister was. 'Twenty-two,' Hamish said. 'She's studying medicine at

London University. She's a candidate in the election, actually. Liberal.'

This information silenced Mr Barnes. He approved of women MPs, but the thought of women doctors made him uneasy.

'Hamish, are you a prefect?' Mrs Barnes asked. 'I meant to ask you before.'

'No, ma'am. I got demoted.'

(*Ma'am!*)

'Some prank?' Molly's dad asked. He liked the thought of that – boys in public schools were supposed to have pranks.

'What did you do?' Molly's mum said.

Hamish smiled modestly and glanced at Molly. 'It was a bit . . .' He hesitated. . . '*explosive*,' he said.

'Ah! Some misdemeanour in the chemistry lab!'

But Hamish had turned to Molly. 'Molly, would you like to come for a walk?' he said. There was no hesitation this time; no pretence that he wanted to talk politics; no chance for her to say she'd fetch her bike. Just a direct question. Hamish had learned his lesson.

Molly looked appealingly at Abigail. 'Will you come?'

But Abigail said no. *It's not me he wants.*

'Adam?'

Adam looked down and shook his head.

Mr Barnes, however, was beaming. 'There's something about that boy,' he said fondly as Molly and Hamish set off for their walk. 'Background, I suppose.'

25

The inside of Adam's head was such a calm place, so steady and fortified, that he observed with amazement the states other people sometimes got into.

There was a boy at his school called Sparkes – Micky Sparkes. He had a truly impressive collection of cigarette cards, about seventy complete sets, with fifty cards in each set. Army badges, flags of the Empire, kings and queens of Britain, famous footballers – that kind of thing. On the last day of term they were allowed to take their hobbies into school. Sparkes had done that, proudly arranging his sets of cigarette cards to display them at their best. A week later, someone stole them, the whole collection. Micky Sparkes was inconsolable. He was in a terrible state – hurt, outraged. He even cried. Other boys were embarrassed by this. Adam was just mystified.

Then there was 'Hoddy' Hodson, whose father beat up his mother regularly. Everybody knew. She was a pale thin woman, often with bruises on her arms and face. Hoddy was a cheerful podgy boy, fourteen years old, untroubled by anything, everyone thought. But one day he turned on his father and beat him up. His dad's face was unrecognisable, people said. Then Hoddy threw him out of the house, ration-book and all. And his dad had gone away, no one knew where.

Adam observed all this with sympathy, but uncomprehending. Where had Hoddy found such passion?

Girls too. There was a girl called Sasha, a lovely-looking girl of sixteen. Lovelier than a film star, people said. She went out with a boy from Ely for about six weeks, told everyone she loved him and they would get married one day. Then the boy went out with someone else. Sasha was heartbroken – not just for a couple of days as you might expect, but endlessly tearful and dispirited. For *months*! Perhaps she *had* really loved that boy.

Adam sensed the turmoil that went on inside people. But he'd felt nothing like that himself.

Until the day his drawings were stolen.

It was impossible that he had mislaid such a large folder with so many drawings in it! *Where did you last put it?* people said to him. Adam nearly went mad with the question. But there were only three possible places: in his bedroom, on the table in the kitchen, or in his desk at school.

But the missing folder was not there. Then they searched in the unlikely places – the barn, the pill-box by the mere, Abigail's house, the garden shed.

Everywhere! They rang the bus company in case he'd left it on a school bus.

Slowly it became impossible to go on believing that the drawings had been carelessly left somewhere and forgotten. They had been taken. *Stolen.*

'All this fuss over some drawings,' Mr Barnes muttered. 'Who'd want them anyway?' Ivy said loudly. Mr Whymper, however, was deeply sympathetic. 'I know how I'd feel if someone stole my postcards,' he said.

The missing drawings included all of Adam's work done in the manner of Picasso, a few Picasso copies, some precious sketches of Molly, and a few of Abigail and little William.

Adam didn't recognise himself. He had no tantrums. There was no shouting, no slamming of doors, nothing like that. Nor did he sulk. Sulking was not part of his nature. He's frozen inside, Molly said to herself. Like Kay in *The Snow Queen*.

He was entirely unresponsive. He wanted nothing from anyone. If they couldn't help him recover his drawings, there was nothing else he wanted from them. He showed no gratitude for the searching that went on.

He stopped drawing. Nothing would induce him to pick up pen or pencil. His current sketchbook lay disregarded. The first pages were crowded with quick experimental sketches, but the rest remained empty.

Mrs Barnes telephoned Adam's art teacher and told

him about it. Unknown to them, Mr Fraser discussed it with his friend, Paterson Royce. Word got about.

They reported the matter to the police and Sergeant Bly dutifully wrote down all the details of the theft. It was now a *theft*. Officially.

The local newspaper heard of the story and sent a reporter. As the reporter came to one door, Adam left by another, leaving Molly's mum to do the talking.

Then there was a phone-call from Hamish. He said he'd read about it in the paper and was there anything he could do to help? Should he cycle over?

Young William avoided Adam now, as if troubled or embarrassed. Adam didn't notice, but Molly did. She told Abigail about it, and Abigail gave William a hug.

Adam's dad came down from London, but he was too harassed by his own work to be much help. Now that the War was over there was a reorganisation of the National Fire Service going on. He had to return on the evening train.

Adam had no interest in any of this concern for him. He remained numb, uncommunicative. No sympathy got through to him. A stranger might not have known he was troubled, but to those who knew him he sent out waves of colourless misery.

On the third afternoon the art teacher and his young wife turned up in their black Austin Seven. Mrs Fraser – unconsciously lovely – kissed Adam.

'He draws her all the time,' Molly whispered to Abigail. 'And does paintings and sculptures.'

'Who? Adam?'

'*No!* Mr Fraser!' Molly had visited the studio. Some of the drawings had made her blush.

They sat in the garden drinking tea. Everyone was there except young William, who had run away and hidden. Mr Fraser said Adam should make a complete list of every drawing that had gone missing. Adam nodded, but he was like a person half in a coma.

Before they left, Mrs Fraser said they were going to call at the police station. 'Why? Do you have any new information?' Mr Barnes asked.

'No,' Mrs Fraser said. 'But I doubt if they fully appreciate the importance of what's gone missing. We can set them straight on that. We mustn't expect the police to understand the importance of this in the way *we* do, Mr Barnes.'

Mr Barnes nodded slowly. *Clever*, Molly thought.

'And if,' Mrs Fraser said as she opened the door of the car, 'the drawings have been stolen, someone must have done it. So why don't you write a list of suspects? Then you can eliminate them one by one.'

Abigail wanted some action. 'Let's do it,' she said when they'd gone. 'Let's write down all the suspects.'

So they started, without much help from Adam.

Mr Whymper. 'He hasn't enough gumption to commit a crime,' Molly said. But he *was* weird, they agreed. So, fully aware of the injustice of this, they

161

put him at the top of the list because he was weird.

Molly's dad. It was Ivy who suggested this. 'Well, he doesn't *like* Adam, that's obvious,' she said. Molly objected, but half-heartedly. So Mr Barnes was added.

Mr or Mrs Fraser. For the first time Adam showed a reaction. He was outraged. 'But they do know about art,' Abigail pointed out.

Mr Paterson Royce. Very little was known about him, but he *was* an art dealer, Molly explained. And Adam had never liked him much.

Professor Beale. Molly was amazed. How could it be *her*? 'She saw Adam's drawings that day at the mere,' Abigail pointed out. 'I'm not saying she did it – just that she should be considered.'

Hamish Macaulay. That was not as silly as it seemed. Hamish, or his friends, might have plotted some kind of practical joke – to annoy Adam. The more they thought about it, the more likely it seemed.

'I'll deal with Hamish,' Molly said. 'Tomorrow.' There was a steely look in her eye.

The list of suspects made no difference to Adam. He didn't believe in it. If his drawings were not found, he thought carefully, it was because they didn't deserve to be. If his friends didn't get them back, it was because they were not real friends. And if his drawings were no good, it would be easier not to try any more. What was the point? What was the point of *anything*?

26

The boys at Greys College were allowed to go into the city after school on market days. Hamish and his friends, Molly knew, liked to have tea at the Etheldreda tea-rooms, close to the cathedral.

So, after school on Thursday, Molly didn't board her school bus but went instead into the city centre. Approaching the tea rooms, she saw at once that Hamish and three of his friends were already there, sitting at a table by the window. Hamish raised a languid hand; the other three just stared.

Molly knew that if she hesitated she wouldn't go in at all. So she made straight for the door, entered, and approached the boys. In their bright purple school blazers they were almost dazzling, resplendent and set apart.

They gazed at her in open-mouthed surprise – except Hamish, who rose at once and greeted her politely.

'Will you join us?' he said. Hamish was the perfect gentleman, cool, tall and unruffled. 'Shawcross Minor, draw up a chair for Molly.'

Shawcross Minor – the smallest of them – dragged a vacant chair from a nearby table. Hamish winced when it squeaked on the floor. Molly sat down, uncomfortably aware that a group of girls from her school, passing by outside, was peering in delight at Molly Barnes having tea with four boys from Greys. Inside, Shawcross Minor couldn't take his eyes off her.

'We're having Earl Grey,' Hamish said loftily.

What is *he talking about?* Molly thought.

'The tea,' Hamish explained.

'Oh,' Molly said. 'Is there some connection with your school?'

'I think not,' Hamish said. 'It's unlikely that there is any connection between our College and a blend of tea.'

'Well, actually . . . '

But Shawcross Minor was told to shut up and the waitress was summoned – a girl who had been in the same class as Molly at primary school. The girl said 'Yes sir' and winked at Molly.

The next ten minutes were awkward. A conversation of sorts managed to limp its way through the tea-drinking. Then, finally, Molly asked Hamish if he would walk with her to the bus stop. 'I have a question for you,' she said. 'It's private.'

The other three eyed each other and made significant faces. 'Pack it in!' Hamish said. 'Or you'll all get scragged.'

Then, to Molly, he said: 'Did you enjoy your tea?'

'Not much. It tasted soapy.'

'It's an acquired taste,' Gulliver murmured. Behind

the counter the waitress stuck her tongue out at him, unnoticed.

Out in the street, Hamish crooked his elbow to invite Molly to take his arm. But Molly walked well clear. If she were seen walking arm in arm with Hamish, it would mean they were practically engaged.

A senior boy from Greys passed by on the other side of the street, grinning. Molly glanced sideways at Hamish and saw that he was blushing fiercely.

But he kept his composure. 'You had something to say,' he remarked.

'Yes.' Molly didn't beat about the bush. 'Was it you that stole Adam's drawings?'

'Certainly not,' he said in his most lordly manner. 'I don't go in for that kind of thing.'

Molly was not to be silenced. 'But what about your friends? *Gulliver*, for example?' Molly disliked Gulliver.

'Gulliver *is* a slimy toad,' Hamish admitted. 'But he certainly hasn't stolen those drawings.'

'How do you know?'

'Because, if he had, he would have shown everyone. He can't help bragging. It's his weakness.'

They walked on. Then Hamish said, 'I say! Is it true that Swales draws pictures of you in the … er …'

Everything was immediately reversed. Molly – who in the tea room had felt like an inferior nobody – became a grown-up woman walking beside a schoolboy.

'Naked?' she asked innocently. Hamish's face, she saw, was flaming again, brighter than before.

Now Molly knew for certain that Hamish hadn't seen Adam's drawings. Mission accomplished, she thought to herself.

'There's my bus,' she said.

Standing on the step of the bus with her season ticket ready, she thanked Hamish for the tea. To her surprise, he put out his hand. She put her hand in his and he solemnly shook it, up and down, very slowly.

Molly couldn't remember having shaken anyone's hand before. It wasn't something she did. But she liked the feel of Hamish's hand.

Well, she thought, now we can remove those public school boys from the list of suspects. The other thing she thought, to her surprise, was that she could still feel Hamish's hand in hers. 'Oh!' she said to herself, with interest.

27

There came a breathless day when too many things happened, and too fast.

It started on the bus after school. Abigail said, 'Do you remember that prisoner-of-war on the train? The one with his hand blown off. Well, I've had a letter from him.'

Molly was all curiosity.

Dear Abigail,
Hello, I hope your OK.

I wanted to write to say thank you for being so kind to me on the train that day.

It was nearly midnight when I got home. Gosh I was tired! But my Mam was waiting up for me and she had my favourite steak and kidney pie keeping warm in the oven. I don't know how she managed to get so much meat, what with rationing.

Everyone is very happy that the war is over but I don't seem able to feel happy about anything. I've lost the knack somehow. Seeing you on that station was the only good thing that's happened to me.

I would like to write to you again. But if it would be a nuisance, I won't.

Yours faithfully,

Harry Dowbiggin

'He doesn't sound very happy,' Molly said.

At Abigail's house, they found her dad had arrived. He was standing at the window, watching for her.

He'd been finally discharged from the army and he was wearing the demob suit that had been issued to him – crumpled, dark blue, creased in the wrong places. The sleeves were too long, the cuffs too big and the collar too large. Everything about him seemed diminished.

'Dad! You're home! Is everything going to be okay now?' It *sounded* all right, Molly thought. But Abigail didn't go over to kiss him. She spoke as if she were being polite to a visitor. And they stayed on opposite sides of the table.

He smiled half-heartedly. 'Yes, the enquiry's over – and I'm not going to be charged with desertion. It was only a formality. I always knew it would be okay. Hello, Molly.'

'Nice to see you, Mr Murfitt,' Molly said. 'How long are you home for?'

Mrs Murfitt came in with some plates. 'One month,' she snapped. 'Then he's going off again!'

'Where to, Dad?'

'Berlin, probably.' It was not the answer anyone expected. As Abigail took it in, he said: 'Abigail, there's a lot to do there. You've no idea. They need help. I've signed on for one more year.'

'And we shall be homeless,' Mrs Murfitt said.

'*Homeless?*'

She leaned across the table, laying out plates, then straightened up. 'The Railway isn't going to let a woman be gatekeeper – not now the War's over. And *he* won't be here! So they'll turn us out and put someone in who's prepared to do the job.' Her voice was like the edge of a saw. She banged down another plate.

Molly watched carefully. Mr Murfitt looked bewildered and lost, like a man in a dream.

'Abigail, who was that letter from – the one you had this morning?'

Abigail brightened a little. 'Do you remember that POW I told you about? The one with only one hand? It's from him.'

'Let me see.' Mrs Murfitt held out her hand.

Abigail hesitated for an instant. But she handed the letter over.

Mrs Murfitt read it and looked up. 'You're not going to answer this,' she said slowly.

'Yes, I am,' Abigail said. 'He means no harm.'

'Abigail, you'll do as you're told! *You are not to answer that letter.*'

It always amazed Molly to see how quickly Abigail's rows blew up. 'Well, that's where you're wrong,' Abigail said. 'And you can't stop me! He was just *unhappy* – and I cheered him up.'

Mrs Murfitt slowly tore the letter into tiny fragments. But Abigail said quietly, 'I've memorised the address.'

'What? Why?'

'Because I *knew* you'd be like this.'

Then Mrs Murfitt turned to her husband. '*You* tell her,' she snapped at him. 'Now you've at last decided to come home, you'd better try and be a father! Tell her she can't be writing letters to strange soldiers. *Deal* with her!'

Mr Murfitt looked helpless. 'How can I deal with her? When I went away, she was ten! *Now* look at her! She's almost grown up.' *You're all strangers!* He didn't say those words, but he might as well have done. They all knew that's what he meant.

Then Ivy came in from work, cheerful because she'd got away early. She stared at Mr Murfitt, not sure who he was. But she did know she'd walked into a row. She pulled a face and rolled her eyes comically. 'Someone's in a *mood*!' she said.

But she got no explanation. They heard the front gate bang and footsteps hurrying towards the house. Molly's mum came straight in through the kitchen.

'Molly, have you seen Adam?'

Molly's blood drained from her face to concentrate on her heart, where it was needed. 'No,' she said. 'What's happened?'

'He's disappeared! I think he's run away.'

28

Frosty spent those early summer months going about his business, always with his overcoat on, belted up tight, even when the weather was warm. One day he got on a bus and went up the West End. He walked the last bit, to Piccadilly Circus.

I suppose they'll put the Eros statue back, he thought. *Now that the bombings have stopped.*

He turned into a backstreet, where there was a cramped little shop called *Ogmore's Art Emporium*. Here, he stood for a few minutes, looking at the pictures in the window – drawings, watercolours, oils, pastels, photos. Some framed, some not.

There were more inside, like the ones in the window – only there were some he wouldn't want to show his old granny if she'd been alive (which she wasn't). They were all over the place – on the wall, on shelves, in stacks.

You could easily fail to notice Mrs Ogmore. She was perched on a stool, motionless, close to a glass case full of art books. She'd hardly ever been known to leave that stool. Even during the daylight air raids she never shifted, people said.

Her voice was husky, like a rusty nail. 'What's up with you?' she growled. 'You look like you've lost a pound and found a tanner!'

'I *am* a bit disappointed, Mrs Ogmore,' Frosty said. 'I hoped you might have some of my stuff in your window. On display.'

'So that's what's given you such a long face! No, your stuff is too good to put on show. I wouldn't put goods like that *on show*!'

Course not, Frosty thought, feeling ignorant. He tried to find out more, but Mrs Ogmore was not a conversationalist. She was known for it. And in any case, another customer came in.

Outside, Frosty stood still for a few minutes, enjoying the sun. But he was in for a shock. There was someone he hadn't noticed, someone small, standing right beside him.

'So she's your new clee-on-tell, is she, Frosty? Well, well, well!'

Frosty's heart sank into his boots.

'You bin selling her some of your fancy shirts?'

Frosty looked unhappy and helpless. 'No, I haven't,' he said. 'And how come you're here?'

'I worry about you, Frosty. I like to keep an eye on my mates.'

Frosty felt one of his small spurts of rebellion coming on. 'Your mates have a habit of turning up early for their funerals,' he muttered.

There was the slightest pause, in which all the sounds

of Piccadilly Circus seemed to be stilled and made dangerous. Impossible, of course, but that's how it seemed to Frosty. *I shouldn't have said that*, he thought.

The Maggot took hold of Frosty's coat collars and pulled him down and close. 'Remember: if you've got anything good, you bring it to *me*! That's the *rule*, Frosty. You don't take it to no one else. That was the mistake Willy Wilson made.'

'I remember you used to call Willy your mate.'

'So he *was*, Frosty, so he was! But he wanted to set up on his own, didn't he? That made him my *rival*. And I don't allow no rivals!'

Frosty could feel the Maggot's breath on his face. Then the older man stepped back and walked off, laughing silently.

29

Molly believed she knew where Adam had gone. They knew he had boarded the school train that morning as usual but, instead of changing at Ely, he'd stayed on the train and travelled on.

There were some frantic phone-calls. It quickly became clear that he had not gone to his grandmother's house in North London, or visited his father at work. Nor had he contacted his mother, who was stationed at an RAF base in Kent.

Abigail suggested that he might have gone to see the art dealer, in search of his missing drawings. So Mrs Barnes phoned Mr Fraser, who phoned Paterson Royce. But no, Adam had not been there.

On the third day, Adam's father phoned. He'd been talking to his sister in North Wales. Adam was not with them – but a solitary boy had been seen wandering in the hills, unkempt and living rough. She was sure this was Adam.

'He loves that place,' Mr Swales said sadly. 'I'm sure that's where he is.'

Molly was sure too. Snowdonia was Adam's other home. He'd spent a lot of time there with his aunt and uncle, and his cousins. It was there – when he was little – that he discovered he could draw.

'He'll turn up when he's ready,' his dad said. But there was anxiety in his voice.

They had to decide whether the police should be asked to begin a search. But Mr Swales was against the idea. 'Let's give him another couple of days.' He knew from his experience in the blitz that missing people usually did turn up. Eventually. 'I don't want him hunted,' he said.

He's not going to be here for my birthday, Molly thought.

She wished she could speak to Adam's aunt or uncle. But she knew, from Adam, that they had no phone and their nearest phone box was two miles away at the end of a lane. However, on the fourth day, Adam's uncle phoned them.

Molly took the receiver off the stem. 'Hello?' She knew who he was the moment she heard his voice. 'I've heard about you,' he said. 'You must be Molly. We got pictures of you all over the place!'

That was news to Molly.

'No, he's not been here. But not to worry – he's been *seen*. People are talkin' about it, and I'm sure it's him.'

The next day Abigail took charge. She sat them down at the big kitchen table to open Molly's birthday presents. And when Molly said sadly, 'I hoped he might send me a birthday card,' Abigail said, 'Come upstairs to your bedroom.'

Little William jiggled up and down with excitement. He had recovered some of his old joyousness.

The four of them hurried out of the kitchen, making a draught and sweeping flat the birthday cards that Molly had carefully stood up on the table.

On Molly's bed was a large brown paper parcel. She stared at it, mystified. 'It's addressed to you,' she said to Abigail.

'It had to come to my house and be hidden there until your birthday.' Abigail felt clever and pleased with herself.

'It's been unwrapped,' Molly said suspiciously.

'Get *on* with it, Molly!' (Sergeant-major Abigail, bossy and kind.)

Inside the parcel was a blue metal case with a handle and a small key in a keyhole. Even before she lifted the lid, Molly knew what was inside. Then she saw it – a brand new portable typewriter with smart white keys and blue trim.

'Gosh!'

A page of foolscap had been inserted in the machine and a message had been typed:

```
For typing up your report about the mediaeval
jetty.

A.
```

Mrs Barnes looked amazed and uneasy. 'It's a lot better than *our* present,' she said.

Molly was fascinated, finger-tipping the keys, sliding the carriage smoothly across, making the bell go ting.

'When did he do this?' Molly asked.

'Oh, weeks ago!' Abigail said airily.

'Your father isn't going to like this,' Mrs Barnes said.

'How could he afford it?' Molly whispered.

Abigail explained. 'He sold some more pictures to Mrs Fraser.'

Abigail the organiser. Sensible, generous.

Abigail! Molly thinks. For there is a disturbance in the gallery, raised voices at the entrance. The interviewer and the film crew look wonderingly at one another. 'Stop filming,' someone murmurs crossly.

It's the second day of the interviewing, and a voice can be heard, raised in irritation. 'I *know* the Exhibition doesn't open until next week!'

Someone says something inaudible.

'*Of course* I'm a member of the public! Aren't *you*?'

She is not to be prevented, this intruder. They hear footsteps approaching the gallery. The door is flung open and she stands there, with a small crowd of gallery staff behind her, irritated and amused.

'Abigail!' Professor Barnes murmurs happily. Tall, dignified, almost stately, Molly crosses the floor to greet her friend. Abigail is also stately and dignified, but

177

smaller, wind-blown, with a blue silk scarf tied round her head like a bandanna. 'I've just flown in,' she says. 'I can't stop, but I wanted to see you. I've a meeting in Amsterdam tomorrow.'

The director of the gallery protests. 'Madam, we can't just let people in here . . .'

'Pay attention!' Abigail says firmly. 'Three of the pictures you're exhibiting belong to me. One more word and I'll take them away with me – *now!*'

A look of recognition passes over the curator's face. 'You're the girl in *Family Reunion!*'

'Is there somewhere to *sit*?' Abigail snaps.

Of course! Molly thinks affectionately. Abigail has spent years terrifying airport officials, politicians, celebrities, soldiers, and chiefs of police – the staff of an art gallery don't stand a chance.

'Molly, it's good to see you,' Abigail says, seated now. She turns to her wider audience. 'I've spent most of my life running charities. They all failed. For lack of money, usually. But one *didn't.* Do you know why? Because Adam Swales gave me one of his paintings to sell and I got half a million for it.'

'What does your charity do?'

'It helps people who get bits of their bodies blown off.'

The television interviewer has an idea. 'Would you let me film you saying that? We could use it.'

Molly half expects a savage answer from Abigail: she's said it once, why should she say it again? But

Abigail is used to giving interviews. 'Yes, of course,' she says. 'Where from? *I've spent all my life running charities*?'

'That will be perfect.'

Molly's granddaughter slips quietly through the bystanders and says, 'Hello.'

A sudden tenderness. 'Hello Carrie,' Abigail says.

Molly says: 'How's Hamish?'

'Bad-tempered,' Abigail says. 'But soldiering on. Everyone takes advantage of his kindness, of course.' Then she says, 'And Adam? Where's he?'

Molly shrugs, sadly.

'Perhaps you'll have to go and find him,' Abigail says. 'You've done it before.'

30

Ever since they'd been about five years old, Molly had watched Abigail's rows with her mum, and Abigail had watched Molly's.

So Abigail recognised the signs, the tone in Molly's voice.

'Mum?'

'What, love?'

'I'm going to Wales.'

'What are you talking about?' Mrs Barnes' voice also gave the game away: she'd half-expected this.

'You *heard* what I said! I'm going to Wales.'

'I can assure you that you're doing no such thing!'

'I've made up my mind. I'm *going*! I'm going to find Adam and bring him back.'

'Molly, what do you take me for? Do you think I'm going to let a fifteen-year-old girl go gallivanting to the other side of the country on her own?'

'*Six*teen.'

'All right, *sixteen*! It makes no difference. You're not going. For heaven's sake, Molly, the trains are full of soldiers!'

'I'll stand if the trains are crowded.'

'That's not what I meant – and you know it. What responsible mum would let her daughter do that?'

'Mum, I've been travelling on trains since I was ten!'

'Not as far as Wales!' Mrs Barnes retorted.

'Come with me, then.'

'You know I can't leave the guesthouse. So let's hear no more about it.'

Forbidden. An absolute veto. That was the end of round one. The next round was most likely to consist of the usual Molly-outrage about unfairness. That was standard practice, Molly's way of surrendering. But once or twice in her life, round two had taken a different turn.

'I'm going, Mum,' Molly said quietly. 'And you can't stop me.'

Mrs Barnes faced Molly across the kitchen table, arms folded, head high. 'Oh can't I!' she said. 'I've told you: *you are staying here, my girl.*'

'I've got enough money for the fare, and I'm going. The only way you can stop me is to lock me up – and I know you won't do that.'

'I don't have to lock you up – you'll just *do what you're told!*'

'You can't guard me every minute of the day,' Molly said.

That marked the end of round two. Mrs Barnes turned back to the cooker and this time she spoke in a different tone of voice. 'Molly, what makes you think Adam *wants* you to find him?' Abigail could see –

though she could hardly believe it – that Molly was going to win.

'He needs help. And I'm the one who can help him.'

'Molly, he can't live *here* any more. And he doesn't *want* to live in London. So he's gone to Wales. He's always said it was one of his favourite places. Besides, you wouldn't know where to start looking. He might be . . .'

In the space left by that unfinished sentence Molly said, 'I'm going, and that's all there is to it! You know you can't physically stop me – so you might as well help and be on my side.'

'What about school?'

'The exams are finished. There are no proper lessons now. I've spent all today pulling weeds out of the tennis courts!'

'But what am I going to tell your father?'

Then Abigail knew the contest was over. Mrs Barnes had lost on points, in three rounds.

'Don't tell him anything,' Molly said quietly.

'*Molly!*' Mrs Barnes stared at her daughter as if she was seeing her for the first time.

'At least, not until after I've gone.'

There was a short pause then, full of waiting.

'Mum, I'm going to do this. But I'd like it best if you were on my side.'

Another silence, full of doubt. Then Mrs Barnes said, 'OK. But there are two rules.'

'Rules?' Molly braced herself for another round.

182

'No, *three*. First, you set off tomorrow morning, not tonight. Second, you promise to phone me every day. *Every* day, mind! And if you haven't found Adam in a week, you come home.'

'I wish I could come too,' Abigail said.

'Molly, promise. *Please.*'

'All right, I promise.'

Mrs Barnes – with amazing adaptability – slipped into organising mode at once. 'Right,' she said. 'You two go to the station now and find out about trains. I'll phone through a telegram to Adam's uncle and ask him to phone me this evening.'

It was almost as if she'd been prepared for this, Abigail thought.

'What for?'

'You'll need somewhere to stay. A bed and breakfast, or a place like ours.'

'He'll probably say I can stay at his farm,' Molly said.

'But we need to know. And I have to find you a decent suitcase. And your blue dress needs ironing.'

Later that evening, Adam's uncle telephoned. No, he said, Adam had not turned up. But Molly was welcome to stay at the farm. 'And we'll meet you at the station – at half-past five, is it?' he added.

There was a thoughtful look on Molly's face as she replaced the phone on its stand. 'What are you looking like that for?' her mother said.

'I think he's glad I'm going.'

I wish *I* was, Mrs Barnes thought. I must be *mad*!

31

It was hardly a valley, more like a small green crease high between mountains. But the western sun was shining on it and Adam, with his back against a rock, had absorbed the warmth and gone to sleep.

But the valley darkened as the sun sank and he awoke in a damp shadowy chill.

There was a dry-stone wall, in front of him. Its stones were mossy and tumbled, buried and overgrown with bracken and grass. There was a flicker of shadow and one of the stones changed into a fox-face.

Watching him.

It wasn't much of a fox. More like a half-starved dog, skinny and wary, with its back arched as it held itself balanced on the wall. Its face was sharp, its look suspicious. One forepaw was lifted and it hung its head low. Its brush was dull and matted. Adam could see patches of dried mud on its side. And a black tear-smear in the corner of each eye.

It's as hungry as I am, he thought. Hunger made Adam muddled and weak, but if a fox was starving, was it confused and dazed? Its legs unsteady? Or did hunger sharpen its skills and make it a more deadly hunter?

When he looked again the fox had turned into Molly Barnes. What was *she* doing there? But she isn't here at all, Adam said sagely to himself. She can't be. And when he concentrated he found he was right. No fox, and certainly no Molly. Just a tumbled dry-stone wall.

When he tried to rise to his feet, he was gripped by a spasm of uncontrollable shivering and fell back against the rock behind him. The difference between me and the fox, he thought at the centre of his headache, is that the fox probably knows where to go in search of something to eat. A hillside farm, perhaps, where there were chickens. He let his eyes close again, wondering if he had the energy to go searching.

'Molly,' Mrs Barnes said.

They were at breakfast, next morning. Molly was restless, agitated, keen to get going.

'About Adam . . .'

Molly paid attention.

'I'm *very* fond of him. Well, you know that. Almost as much as if he were my own son – which is stupid, because he isn't.'

Molly felt herself going rigid with resistance. 'What are you trying to say, Mum?'

'I'm trying to say that I like him, but I don't have any illusions about him – and I don't think you should have any either. I don't think he's entirely . . .' she hesitated '. . . *reliable*.'

'What do you mean, *not reliable*?'

'I mean that he likes putting you in his pictures,' Mrs Barnes said. 'He likes *drawing* you – but that's all, probably.'

'Oh, I know that,' Molly said. 'I must get going.'

I will never understand my daughter, Mrs Barnes thought.

Abigail, feeling lonely, wrote the forbidden letter, to her ex-POW. After two paragraphs of chat, she concluded –

I think it would be better if you don't write to me any more. It's not that your letters would be a nuisance. (He ought to learn how to spell that word, she thought.) *It's just that I'm still a schoolgirl and my mum thinks I shouldn't be getting letters from a man I don't really know.*
Yours sincerely,
Abigail Murfitt.

She felt cruel, writing that, so she added –

P.S. But if you feel desperate, write anyway.

Her dad had agreed with her mum, but for different reasons. 'He'll become dependent on you,' he explained. 'The biggest kindness you can do for him is not to let him.'

So she showed her reply to him and he approved of it, except for the postscript.

'But it seems so cruel!' Abigail said.

'It would be a lie.'

'A *lie*?'

'If he really gets desperate, you couldn't help him anyway. You're too inexperienced. And too far away.'

Abigail took to heart what her father had said and rewrote the letter, without the PS.

Mr Murfitt took to going on long walks every evening. He would set off along the river bank, silhouetted against the sky, walking for miles in those long summer evenings.

Abigail went with him sometimes. She knew he was not seeing the flat fields and wide skies around him. His vision was somewhere else, where there were homeless families without food, cities annihilated by our bombers, Frenchmen who'd collaborated with the Nazis too frightened to go home, terrified French girls who'd had babies with German boyfriends, lost Jewish children looking for their families, German soldiers who had fled their units. There was no work, insufficient food, thousands of refugees, confused and scared. This was what he saw and what he was going back to.

I wish I could go with him, she thought. Then, with a quickening of her heartbeat: do I *really* wish that?

32

Molly was taken aback by the loveliness of the mountains of North Wales. She felt changed by them, transformed. There was an unfolding, a recognition, as if something inside her had been waiting to find them.

She had a compartment to herself. As the train wound its way slowly up beside the River Conwy she hurried eagerly across from one open window to the other. The valley was lush and rich, in bright and shadowy green. Even the air seemed different, moist and soft. The smoke from the engine wrapped itself softly around tree trunks, or carefully arranged itself in layers above the surface of the river.

Molly knew this didn't count as going abroad. Still, Wales was its own country, and it wasn't England. *And*, she thought, *I've made this journey on my own.*

Adam had told her once that this was where he'd first learned to *see*, and where he first wanted to draw.

She heard the engine whistle and the next moment the train was in a tunnel. Smoke swirled into the compartment. In total darkness Molly closed one of the windows and then felt her way to the other side and shut the other.

The tunnel seemed endless. It must have taken five full minutes to get through it. Then the train swung round a wide bend and stopped at Molly's station.

She opened the door and a smart young woman reached in for her case. 'I'm Gwen,' she said. 'Adam's cousin.'

Molly suddenly felt shy, and the absurdity of what she was doing struck her. But Gwen put her at her ease, chatting calmly as she led Molly out of the station. The train pulled away and the sudden silence was filled with the gentle bleating of thousands of sheep.

Gwen threw the case into the back seat of a dark blue Ford 8 and told Molly to get in.

'Do you work on the farm?' Molly asked.

Gwen smiled and shook her head. 'Heard of the National Gallery in London?' she said. 'I work for them. At the start of the War they moved all their paintin's up here. Under a mountain for safety. I got a job with them and I've stayed with them ever since.'

'Under a mountain?' It sounded like a fairy story.

'Yes. So Adam didn't tell you, then? It was supposed to be top secret, but he found out when he was about eleven. I made him promise not to tell.'

'He never breathed a word,' Molly said.

Gwen nodded. 'He's good at silence.'

Molly adjusted her assumptions. These people knew Adam differently. He belonged to them too. 'What will you do when the paintings go back to London?'

'Oh, I'm goin' with them,' Gwen said. 'I know what

189

you're thinkin'. What it is, see, I've had enough of Wales for a bit. Anyway, my mum's a Londoner and I'm half London myself. If I don't like it, I'll come back.'

Molly wanted to know how Adam's London aunt had come to fall in love with a Welsh hill farmer, but she was too shy to ask. Instead, she asked if there'd been any more news about Adam.

'No. A boy's been seen wanderin', but that's all we know. Have his drawin's turned up?'

Molly shook her head. 'Everyone's baffled,' she said.

Gwen turned the car into a narrow lane that led steeply up the mountainside. There was a phone-box at the corner. 'How far is it now?' Molly asked.

'Only a couple of miles.'

'Oh!' Molly said. 'Your dad had to come all the way down here and all the way back again whenever he phoned us.' She was remorseful.

'Don't you worry about him,' she said. 'He came down on the tractor.'

There was a stone cottage tucked into the hillside. Nothing else for miles. Adam could see the outline of the roof and a chimney stack against the sky.

The black of the night was turning grey. Dawn was approaching.

There was a gap in the wall, with an open iron gate, sunk into the wet grass.

He went in cautiously and walked around the side of

the house to the back. Not a garden, just a grassy enclosure. There were some low stone buildings and in one of them something stirred heavily, and grunted.

Pigs. They kept pigs. He could smell them – a mixture of straw, urine and dung. Chickens too, probably. He stood for several minutes, looking intently at the back of the house, especially the windows. Not a sound, not a movement.

He found the back door and quietly lifted the latch. The door was unlocked. Inside, he was in a large kitchen. In the grey dawn he could make out a table, a black range against the opposite wall, a stone sink and a slate draining board under a low window.

On the draining board stood a pie on a dish. Round and tall, a pork pie probably. Beside it was a long sharp knife. His hunger was acute, desperate. It immediately became obsessed with that pie. He took two steps forward.

Then someone spoke.

A sharp fierce voice, speaking Welsh. For all he knew there might be a shotgun aimed at him in the shadows.

He stood motionless. A match was struck and applied to an oil-lamp. The flame ran round the circular wick, the glass chimney was fitted, and a large transparent globe placed over it.

The kitchen was illuminated, the match extinguished. A woman stood there looking at him. In a long brown dressing-gown and wellington boots. Her grey hair was bound in a plait.

She spoke again, in Welsh. Accusing, angry.

'English,' he said. His voice croaked.

The woman looked him up and down. She was fearless, despite his appearance. 'Run away, have you?' she said in Welsh-English.

He nodded.

'Hungry,' she said.

It was a statement, not a question. Again Adam nodded. There were no more questions. She indicated a wooden chair and told him to sit at the table. Then she busied herself, without speaking. A mug of sweet tea arrived almost at once, but the rest he had to wait for. Sausages, fried eggs, fried bread, bacon and some thick slices of bread-and-dripping. She prepared three plates, one for him, one for her. 'My husband,' she said, when she saw him looking at the third.

She reminded him of someone, he couldn't remember who.

She put one of the plates and a drink on to a tray and carried them out of the kitchen. He heard her mounting the stairs somewhere. Then low voices in the room above.

When she came down, she went outside to let the chickens out. Back inside, she took off her boots and sat down to her own breakfast, eating quietly.

When he'd finished she gave him more bread. The fried food had all gone. He had two more mugs of tea. Overwhelmed by exhaustion, he pushed his empty plate aside and laid his head on his arms.

But she shook his shoulder. He had already plunged into sleep, but she dragged him back and pointed to a sofa along one wall. He rose reluctantly and almost fell across it.

'Take your shoes off!' she said. 'Where were you brought up?'

Wearily he stooped and pulled off his filthy shoes. There was a cushion for his head, but his legs had to be drawn up to allow for his length. The last thing he saw as he sank into unconsciousness was her farm-worn fingers pulling apart his muddy shoelaces.

He awoke after several hours. The kitchen was flooded with soft grey daylight. The woman – dressed now – was cooking, and the clock on the mantelpiece said almost one o'clock.

He needed to pee but was too shy to ask. It was urgent. But she knew without being told. She pointed to a dark door, under the stairs. There was no toilet, just a chamber pot and a bowl of water on a small table. There was no light, so he had to leave the door open. He washed his face and hands, and wondered where to empty the pot.

He carried it into the kitchen. She indicated outside, where there was a drain beside the open door. There was a water-butt, and he was going to rinse the pot in it, but from the kitchen door she said No, and pointed to a small pipe in a grassy bank where a stream of hill water trickled.

He sat at the table and watched her. Again three

plates. Rabbit and gravy, leeks and mashed potatoes.

'Is your husband coming . . . ?'

She answered in Welsh, then corrected herself. 'He won't be coming down,' she said. 'He's on his last legs.'

The rabbit was full of bones, but delicious. There was a second helping. Then spotted dick and treacle.

Afterwards she cut a big slice of the pork pie and wrapped it in greaseproof paper. Then she washed out a bottle with a screw-top lid and filled it with milk.

'I don't want to see you here again. Understand?'

It was a bargain.

He put the pie in one pocket and the bottle in the other. 'Thank you,' he said.

She came out with him and stood at the gate to watch him leave. Should he go up the lane? Or back the way he'd come? It made no difference, since he had no destination.

He looked back once. The woman had gone inside, and the house stood silent in the grey light.

Then Adam remembered who she reminded him of. It was his art teacher's young wife, Mrs Fraser. The two women were not at all alike, but they had that same look, unhurried and straight-backed, focused.

It occurred to him then that it was several weeks since he'd thought about drawing. That had never happened to him before. He felt lost, bereaved.

33

They were in their usual café, off Mercer Lane market. Bob and Dolly Swales, sharing tea and biscuits. She'd come up to town for the day. She did that from time to time.

'Should we be worried about him?' Dolly asked.

Bob shook his head. 'I don't think so. Still, if he hasn't shown up by the weekend, I'll take a few days off and go up to Wales. And I'll get every copper they've got looking for him!'

'It's a big area to search.'

'It is, but a stranger wandering about those hills will be spotted by the locals. He'll stand out a mile.'

'Bob . . .' she said.

But he interrupted her. 'It's Hitler's fault. If we'd stayed together as a family, the three of us, none of this would've happened.'

She tried again. '*Bob!*'

'We got to start making plans for the future, Dolly. Everything's going to be different now. By the way, I've put our name down for one of them new apartments they're building.'

Bob's hands were knuckled over one another on the

table in front of him. Dolly leaned forward and placed her hand on his. 'Bob,' she said, 'There's something I've got to tell you.'

Bob sighed. 'I thought there might be.' He waited, looking affectionately at her.

34

The telephone kiosk at the bottom of the hill became a red marker in Molly's life.

Adam's aunt had written down the times of the buses. One went every morning more or less in the right direction – among the hills and along the valleys where people had seen a boy living rough. So every morning Molly boarded the bus and each day she got off at a more distant stop.

The same bus, with the same driver and conductor, dropped her at the same place every evening at six-thirty-five. That was when she phoned home, as promised. *No, I haven't found Adam yet.* She always dealt with that first. *But they're all so kind!* Tears came into her eyes as she tried to make her mum understand. *Everyone here is so nice to me! No wonder Adam loves being here!*

Soon, people would start to worry about his safety. She knew that. But Molly never thought he would come to any harm. She couldn't believe that innocent and beautiful countryside would hurt him. Besides, he was the kind of boy who could look after himself. *Finding* him was what mattered, not *saving* him.

Every evening Adam's other cousin, Bronwen,

would arrive on her motorbike. She worked in the town library, and on her way home from work she stopped by the phone box to give Molly a lift up the lane. Slowly the overloaded machine spluttered its way up the winding hill until its engine died with relief in the slatey farmyard.

But on the fifth evening, Molly was not on the bus. It stopped, however, and the conductor had a word with Bronwen.

There is nobody else in the world.

She is making her way along a track, sunk deep between walls of stone that seem to have grown out of the ground over thousands of years. She meets a small herd of cows, seven of them, with swollen udders urgent for milking. The leader eyes her nervously, swings up her big head and churns clumsily past, lashing her tail. The others follow. Round a bend comes a dog, a collie trotting along, not working, just there for company. Behind the dog, an old man, herding the cows.

Has he seen a boy? Wandering about in the hills? But he answers her in Welsh. She has her hand on his sleeve, to keep him there. She shows him a photograph in the fading light, and he nods slowly and beckons her to go with him.

After about half a mile, he points along a grass-grown trackway.

The evening is warm and still. The track takes her over the breast of a hill and into a steep tiny valley where there is a small lake, almost imprisoned by dark crags towering above it.

No stir of air is there. She stops, seized by its loveliness. A small stream, white and soft-voiced, quietly falls into the lake on the far side. At one end, the surface of the water is gently feathered. But the rest is black and still, a perfect mirror.

The sort of lake that you see in dreams.

She remembers that a man she once knew had told her that if you looked into still water at twilight you'd see the reflections of the stars before you could see them in the sky. She wonders if that's true.

A tiny bird shoots across the surface of the lake, making a line of small circular ripples. And another, from the same place. And another. Yet she never actually *sees* the birds.

In the darkest corner of the lakeside, someone is playing ducks-and-drakes, skimming flat pieces of slate across the water. One of them almost reaches the middle of the lake before it sinks.

A cold finger strokes her back, from between her shoulder blades to the base of her spine.

His lifelong passion has deserted him.

His mind used to be like a shoal of silver fish that darted out into the world as he saw it, peering into light and shade, swimming eagerly among the lovely folding depths and distances.

No eager little fish now. Planes and curves, colour and form, have liquefied into something meaningless, with no colour and no interest. Once or twice, he has briefly thought something worth drawing; but before the thought forms itself, it turns into something trivial, not worth the effort of trying.

He skims another piece of slate and wonders if the first one he threw – half an hour ago – has reached the bottom yet. These lakes are said to be immensely deep. Idly he speculates: if he sat here skimming stones for a hundred years, would they gradually build up to a small island in the middle of the lake?

There is someone on the far side of the water. This irritates him. His unhappiness is too serious to be interrupted. He doesn't want his despair to be intruded upon.

When he realises who she is he inwardly turns away, rejecting.

There has been – ever since it happened – something knotted inside him. He is precise about it. It's in his chest, about two inches below his throat. He almost *feels* it shift and loosen itself, as if he is about to gulp up some knotted wormlike thing.

There is no path around the lake, just a tiny beach of black scree. She scrunches slowly round, scrambling among a thousand-year-old tumble of fallen boulders, and picking her way among tussocky bog-grass.

The dream comes to an end about here. It turns into something that has to be dealt with.

He stares at the water, not looking at her as she approaches. 'Shove up,' she says, and he moves along so that she can sit beside him on the rock.

She has things to say to him. She has practised them in her head. There is a sermon on how badly he has worried all the people who care about him. And a practical argument that he's lost only two or three years' worth of work and that he has, probably, fifty more years to get on with.

But none of these things gets said. 'Look at the state of your trousers,' she says, 'and what's happened to your left shoe?' There is much more she might have commented on. He is in a terrible state.

His voice sounds strange to her. And to him. 'I lost it in a bog.'

His foot is filthy and it's been bleeding. She picks up a flat stone and skims it. Elegantly, it leaps across the lake until it subsides and disappears. Then he picks one up too and in silence they both skim more of the stones. She is better at it than he is; she is better at a lot of things. She briefly wonders if she should let him skim further than she does. Just this once. But she refuses to fake failure.

One of the stones waterskis right to the centre of the lake, lost in the shadows. But neither knows which of them threw it.

'Come on,' she says, getting to her feet. 'It's almost dark.'

He stands, exhausted and dizzy with hunger, and begins to follow her, limping.

There is a long and uncomfortable walk around the lake, along the trackway, then into the lane. It is completely dark when they pass the small farmhouse where the old man lives with his dog and his seven cows. She hopes their udders are empty now and they are at peace for the night.

Where the lane joins the road, there is – what a relief! – a telephone box. She has enough coppers to phone home, enough phone-time to tell her mum that she's found Adam. Mrs Barnes will phone his dad.

But there is no way of phoning his uncle at the farm. They have a nine mile walk ahead of them. She despairs, almost, as she comes out of the telephone kiosk. He is sitting on the grassy-brackenny bank at the roadside, clasping his knees and with his head down. Asleep, probably, but she grabs his arm and hauls him up.

'I thought it would help,' he says, 'coming here.'

She dislikes his pathetic tone. It sounds like a stranger. 'You should have tried *me*!'

In the dark distance of the night she hears the sound of a tractor. No lights. Here, the blackout has become a habit. The sound rises and fades as it climbs over ridges and drops into valleys. But it is drawing nearer, no doubt about it.

Then it comes into sight, a shapeless block of movement on the dark road.

She shouts some eager meaningless thing.

The reply comes back. 'Is that you, Molly?'

It is Adam's Uncle Hugh, come to look for her. A mucky wooden trailer is attached to the back of the tractor. 'Come on, you! A bit bumpy it will be, but better than walking.'

Molly climbs in after Adam, struck by how gentle and kind his uncle is. He really must love Adam, she thinks.

Then it becomes dreamlike again. Adam falls asleep, leaning against Molly. And Uncle Hugh sings *Bread of Heaven* at the top of his voice, drowning out the tractor, all the way home.

Or did she dream that?

35

'Molly! There's a letter for you!'

Adam, standing behind her in his pyjamas, rested his chin on her shoulder and read it with her. It was from Abigail.

Dear Molly,

I'm glad you've found Adam. You've been there long enough! I need you back here. There is SOMETHING GOING ON!

A crowd of girls at school — Pauline Smith and Aggie Roberts and that lot — have been telling me things about Ivy. I couldn't believe what they were saying! They all live in Ely and they say she's got a boyfriend! I could hardly believe it — after all, she's married! But I couldn't tell them that. They say Ivy's been seen in Ely lots of times with this man. They often go to the Rex together. And he's not so much a boyfriend, more a MANfriend cos he's a lot older than she is. And Lizzie Raynham says she saw them kissing on Ely station!

What am I to do, Molly? If I tell Mum, she won't think there's any harm in it. Because she doesn't know Ivy's married. HELP!

Lots of love and hugs,

Abigail.

PS Bring him home soon.

Molly folded the letter and put it away. Abigail and Ivy, Mr and Mrs Murfitt, her own mum and dad, everyone at Great Deeping – they were tiny matchstick figures in a country as far away as China.

'Today,' Adam said, 'I'm taking you to see Betsy.'

'Who's Betsy?'

Adam's aunt called from the kitchen. 'He's pulling your leg, Molly. It's not a person, it's a place. Betys-y-Coed. It's lovely round there! Go and get dressed, Adam, and I'll make you both some sandwiches.'

Adam had slept a lot. Then he'd eaten a lot. He'd quickly regained his strength and his appetite, and his cheerfulness too. But not his interest in drawing.

Molly wrote to Abigail.

I found the boy, but the artist is still lost.

As they approach the summit, Adam takes Molly's hand and helps her up. There is a small plateau, high and flat and grassy, with a cool wind. She is breathless and sticky.

Below them is a wide brilliant valley, filled with sunlight. Cloud-shadows slide across the opposite hillside and a faint clatter of running water rises from the rocky stream that flows along the bottom. Below them a big dark bird circles slowly with an occasional bleak cry.

The hillside falls steeply from their feet to the valley bottom. Like a roof. Too steep for walking or running.

Certainly too steep for safety. But Adam looks at Molly, a challenge, an invitation.

Molly is fearful. 'We couldn't,' she says. 'We'd fall forward and smash our heads on a rock.' There are sharp outcrops, boulders, sinister patches of scree.

But her body is sweaty and overheated, and her skin is prickly with bits of grass, heather stems and bracken dust. The river below looks clean and inviting.

Adam takes her hand again. 'Dig your heels in hard. *And don't lean forward!*'

Recklessly they begin the descent, a mad kind of movement, knees bent like sprung hinges, shoulders forcing their weight backwards, hands clasped.

It is exciting, scary, completely crazy. Partly running, partly heel-skating. Mostly out of control.

It's impossible to stay together. Adam goes ahead, then brakes and stops, breathless. Then it is Molly who goes ahead, slowing herself down, pressing herself back onto the hillside.

The inevitable happens. She trips over a projecting rock – but manages to throw her body into a sideways sprawl and save herself from falling headlong. Gasping and shaken, she rights herself and carries on down, slowing occasionally by sliding on her behind.

Adam's foot sinks into a hole, hidden and boggy. He trips, falls violently forward, and keeps himself upright only by moving his legs at an impossible speed. Molly grabs his flying shirttail as he staggers past her, to steady herself and to save him from falling forward.

Weight and momentum are beginning to defeat their efforts. But at last the slope gentles as they come into the valley-bottom. Adam, however, is going too fast to stop. Or perhaps he doesn't want to stop. He crashes noisily into the boulder-strewn river and falls headlong.

Molly is more circumspect, shakily stone-stepping across the flashing water. When she finds a flat boulder, sturdy and reliable in mid-stream, she stops and bends over, gasping, with her hands on her knees, until she's got her breath back. Every bit of her is trembling, her heart is pounding, and her legs and knees keep wanting to give way. Then she turns to Adam and reaches out for his hand.

'What happened?'

It was more than sixty years ago, this story. Yet Molly's granddaughter is anxious. Interviewer, film crew, even the mics and cameras – all seem to be spellbound.

Molly briefly touches the child's head, reassuringly. 'I pulled him out,' she says. 'Or he pulled me in. One or the other.'

The cameras home in on a picture, a painting in oil. It has become famous, reproduced a thousand times, in books, on posters, on tablemats.

'The girl in the picture, she *is* you?'

The girl in the drawing stands, half in profile, looking across the bare water of a lake surrounded by dark mountains. On the other side, hardly visible in the shadows, is a fox. They seem to recognise each other, the girl and the fox, but you can't be sure.

When Molly remembers this, it is always like recalling a dream.

36

'The thing about Adam's mum is that she . . .' Mr Swales frowned a little, seeking the right words, 'she *bursts out!*' he declared. 'In ways no one is expecting.'

It was Molly Mr Swales kept looking at as he talked, as if he thought she might understand what he only half-understood himself.

He shook his head thoughtfully. 'At the start of the War she joined the WAAFs. She wanted to do her bit, just like everyone else. But *now* look what she's decided to do!'

On their journey back from Wales Adam and Molly had come via London to meet Mr Swales for tea. So there they were, in Lyons' Corner House on Tottenham Court Road. The menu wasn't as good as it was in pre-war days, Mr Swales said. But it looked pretty good to Adam and Molly, who had had nothing to eat since breakfast.

'She likes it, you see. She likes being a WAAF, and she's done really well. She's been made up to Captain.'

He shook his head and chuckled in a would-you-believe-it way. 'Most of them will be demobbed now that the War's nearly over. But she wants to stay and make a life of it! Would you Adam-and-Eve it? – she's signed on for another five years!'

Three peach melbas arrived. 'We've only just started serving these,' the waitress said. 'First time since 1940!'

'You see, Molly, I had hoped that when the War was over we could get one of those flats the government is going to build; and be a family again. You know – just the three of us. I said that to her, but she just said, *Bob*, she said, *Bob! Think about it! By the time they've built those flats*, she said, *Adam will be eighteen or nineteen. He'll be leaving home!* She's quite right – she usually *is*. Still . . .'

Molly wanted to cuddle him. He was not angry or hurt; just baffled by the way things were turning out.

'Adolf Hitler has done that to us,' Mr Swales said. 'He didn't manage to kill any of us three, but he's taken away our life as a family.'

'But you did have ten years of family life before the War, when Adam was little,' Molly pointed out.

'Time's a funny thing, Molly,' Mr Swales said. 'During the bombing, I've looked up sometimes at a building that was going to come down. Ten or twelve storeys high. And from the time it starts to topple until the dust blows away might take p'raps less than a minute. But when you're watching, it seems to take a hundred years! But those ten years before the War went in the blink of an eye!'

He stirred his tea thoughtfully. 'So if your mum is going to stay in the forces,' he said to Adam, 'you might as well stay where you want to be. Because we ain't going to be able to live together anyway.'

Molly felt her heart speeding up.

'So I've been down to Great Deeping and I've fixed it up with your mum, Molly. And Adam is to stay with you. Not as an evacuee, mind – that's all finished – but as a paying guest.'

'Until I take the Lower School Cert?'

'No, until you take your Highers as well. I've been to our local council and they will go on paying your scholarship.'

'That's very kind of them,' Molly said.

'Not really. They were grateful. Most of the schools in East London have been flattened. Adam's one person less to find a place for. But they won't pay any extras, mind, like train fares.'

Molly watched Adam, absorbing this.

'And I also went to see your art teacher as well. He doesn't expect to teach much longer, with younger men coming out of the forces. Poor blighter – he's over seventy! But he says you can go and work in his studio as often as you want.'

Adam stared in disbelief at the way things were turning out. An unworthy thought occurred to Molly: would Mr Fraser die before he'd taught Adam everything? And in any case would Adam be interested now that he'd stopped drawing?

She looked at Adam, in search of clues. But the conversation took a different turn.

'I met his wife too,' Mr Swales said. Molly knew

what was coming next. It always did. 'Lor, she's a corker and no mistake!' He shook his head in disbelief that any woman could be so stunning.

'Now, Molly. I'd like you to leave us alone for a few minutes, if you don't mind. There's something I need to say to Adam.'

Molly was sometimes slow on the uptake. She was halfway down the stairs – feeling confused and embarrassed – before she realised that Adam was going to get a telling-off.

Outside, in Tottenham Court Road, she walked slowly towards where the *Barrel of Beef* had once been. The road and the pavements had been cleared weeks ago, but the mountains of rubble were still there, where the V-2 had exploded. Someone had painted *HITLER'S FINAL FLING* on a wooden board. She walked down the side street to Hamish's coin shop, still open for business but with the window boarded up. *I wonder if they've got their new lav*, she thought.

The sky was empty now; a safe sky over Britain.

Twice she went back to the café and twice she saw across the crowded room Mr Swales talking earnestly to Adam, who was looking down at his empty plate and saying nothing. On the third occasion she met them coming out. They'd finished, apparently. Adam gave her a grin, bleak and a bit helpless.

'Have you ever been in a London taxi, Molly?' Mr Swales said brightly.

Molly had never been in *any* taxi.

'Right! We'll take a taxi to Liverpool Street Station, and I'll see you off.'

That afternoon, Paterson Royce locked up his gallery and set off to Piccadilly Circus.

He disliked Ogmore's Art Emporium. He found the pictures there unpleasant and vulgar. But Edna Ogmore had phoned him for advice. Besides, she had a fine eye for a work of art. Her judgement was rarely wrong.

'Mr Royce! It's a pleasure to see you.'

'You said you're worried about some drawings.'

'Picasso,' she said.

He was instantly interested. 'You have one?' he asked.

'I have four!'

'*Four!* May I see them?'

Mrs Ogmore eased herself up from her stool and led Paterson Royce into a small back room behind a curtain. This room, too, was filled with drawings, but it was tidier. Many an expensive purchase had been made there.

'Suddenly every collector wants a Picasso!' Edna said. 'I had seven to start with and I've sold three already. But now I'm worried.'

'You think they might not be quite tickety-boo?' Mr Royce asked. He sat down at the desk. The four drawings were laid out in front of him.

'They ain't prints,' Mrs Ogmore said.

'They're not Picassos either,' Mr Royce said softly. 'What about the paper?'

'French,' she said. 'So if they ain't Picassos, they could be by one of his mates.'

'Not necessarily. A good counterfeiter would take the trouble to get the right paper.'

'So you think they're fakes?'

Paterson Royce took out a magnifying glass. He peered in silent concentration. 'It's more complicated than that. See – they're signed.'

In each drawing there was a minute monogram – a capital A and a capital S overlaid one above the other so that the centre part of the S formed the cross-stroke of the A. They were so tiny that they might have been put in with the point of a needle. And each was at the end of a line in the drawing – a drape, a hair, a fingernail. There would be nothing like that in a Picasso.

'AS or SA,' Edna Ogmore said. 'I missed that. Do you know who the artist is?'

'I might. Who sold you these, Edna?'

'I can't tell you,' she said.

He looked askance at her. 'No, it's the truth. He wouldn't give his name. Big bloke, wearing a winter coat. Come in a few weeks ago with seven of these drawings.'

Paterson Royce frowned.

'He's been back once, to collect his cash.'

'Have you ever seen him before?'

She shook her head. 'But I can tell you one thing, Mr

Royce – he didn't know nothing about art. You could see that. But word is getting about, see. People are starting to realise that if they spend a hundred pound on a Picasso now they'll get a thousand in five years' time. You can't blame 'em.'

'I need to take these, Edna.'

'They're dodgy?' She sounded resigned.

'I think they've been stolen.'

'A police matter?'

'It might be, it just might be.'

Paterson Royce took a taxi back to his gallery. Inside, he left the CLOSED notice in place and arranged the four drawings on his table. But he couldn't concentrate on them. His real interest was centred on the mysterious package that had arrived by post a few days ago – a large envelope with two bits of cardboard to stiffen it, crudely cut with scissors. And between the cards a pen-and-ink drawing of a girl, naked, seated in a shadowy bedroom, with a streetlight softly glowing in the darkness outside her window.

Pure Picasso! And yet it wasn't. It had taken his breath away.

There was no message inside, no note, no clue. So who had sent it? And why? And why to *him*?

He knew he should phone Scotland Yard. But first he wanted to speak to his schoolmaster friend, Peter Fraser, down in the country.

'Peter? It's Paterson.'

'Hello old chap! How are you?'

'Peter. That boy you've been teaching. What's his surname?'

'Swales. He's Adam Swales.'

'Have his missing drawings turned up yet?'

'No, not as far as I know.'

'Were they Picasso copies?'

'Not *copies*. He did his own.'

'His own what?'

'Drawings in a Picasso manner.'

'How many?'

'He doesn't know exactly. But there must have been about fifty.'

'*What?*'

'The boy was gripped by him. For several months.'

'I see. Peter, what kind of paper do you use?'

'French mostly. I bought stacks of it in Paris before the War. Drove home with a car-load.'

'Does anyone else use it?'

'Marion does, of course. And Adam. I let him help himself when he needs some.'

Paterson Royce rang off. He was glad the pupil hadn't been sneakily stealing his master's best paper.

Molly's father was at Great Deeping station to meet them. She hadn't expected that. Mr Barnes took her case and kissed her. 'I'm glad you're all right,' he said to Adam over Molly's shoulder.

But Molly couldn't make sense of him. He was as

restless as a fidgety child. His face was transfigured with excitement. 'I *told* you!' he said triumphantly. 'And you wouldn't believe me!'

'Believe what?' (*Perhaps he doesn't know. Perhaps Mum never told him.*)

'The *news*! It's *amazing*!'

'*What* news?' (*But he wouldn't be at the station to meet me if he hadn't known I'd been away.*)

'Labour has won the election! The results have been declared – and Churchill's out!'

Molly's mind flash-backed to London – she'd half-noticed people in groups talking eagerly, studying newspapers in the streets, some sadly shaking their heads, others agog and rapt.

As they walked towards the town Mr Barnes told them all about it. Only a couple of days ago Mr Churchill had been at an international meeting with Josef Stalin and Harry Truman. They'd sent a message to the Japanese government threatening prompt and utter annihilation unless they surrendered at once.

Prompt and utter annihilation, Molly thought, wonderingly. What does *that* mean?

'Mr Churchill flew home to find that he'd been voted out. Think of it, Molly! From now on you'll be able to go to the doctor when you're ill – no matter how poor you are. No more doctor's bills! And *no more wars!*'

To Molly, it came as an immediate change of atmosphere, a change in the air. Britain was exactly the same as it had been before; yet everything was different.

Despite her sympathy for poor Mr Churchill, Molly felt a heart-lift of excitement. Something new was starting.

Adam asked if Mrs Barnes was at home. Then he sprinted off ahead of them. Molly watched his rucksack bouncing on his back. *He's going to say sorry*, she thought, approving.

'Dad . . .' she said. 'Molly . . .' Mr Barnes said at the same moment.

She gave precedence to him. 'Your mum was wrong to let you go off like that.'

She waited. (*I wish he'd start drawing again.*)

'To go gallivanting all over the country! On your own, at your age!'

'I'm sixteen.' (*Suppose he never does.*)

'You know what I mean.'

'I came to no harm.' (*Is there any way I could make him?*)

'Maybe not. But if I'd been at home, you wouldn't have gone. I wouldn't have allowed it.'

(*You wouldn't have been able to stop me.*) 'How's William?'

'And that's another thing! As soon as he knew you were coming home, he started behaving . . . I don't know, as if he's *scared* of something.'

37

A man she'd never seen before came into Mrs Ogmore's shop. He was smartly dressed. Small and dapper, with watchful eyes.

The Maggot looked about him, his hands in his coat pockets. 'You the proprietor?' he said.

'Who wants to know?'

'*I* want to know.'

'And who are you?'

This was getting him nowhere. So the Maggot took the bull by the horns. 'I have reason to believe . . .'

Edna Ogmore laughed throatily. 'You sound just like a copper!'

The Maggot drew himself up a little. 'I have reason to believe that one of my men has been selling you stuff illegally.'

'*Illegally*? So did this *stuff* belong to you?'

The Maggot frowned his contempt for that question. 'That's got nothin' to do with it! He sells stuff to *me* – and not to no one else, understand?'

'I don't think that's any concern of mine,' Mrs Ogmore said quietly.

'It *is* your concern if it's you he's bin dealin' with! I

know he's bin here. I want to know what he sold you.'

'*Do* you?'

'Yes, and I intend to find out.'

'Who was he?'

'Tall man, always wears an overcoat. Even in hot weather.'

'I can't think who he could be,' Edna said softly.

'I want to know what he sold you. And I want to know *now*.'

Still speaking very quietly, Edna said she never discussed her business affairs with other people.

'I don't think you quite understand,' the Maggot said slowly. 'When my men play clever tricks with me, they get to be made very sorry. They get *hurt*.' Then he added, 'And anyone they've dealt with gets to wish they hadn't.'

The Maggot moved his right hand and slipped it inside his left sleeve, and Edna – who had been brought up hard in the London Docks – spotted this. She didn't hesitate. She moved her right hand down behind her stool to where there was a round bell-push fitted on the wall. She pressed it, hard.

Immediately there was a movement in the next room, the curtain was swept aside and a burly young man walked soundlessly in and stood quietly beside Edna. Almost as quickly there were sounds of heavy footsteps on a staircase and two more men appeared through an unnoticed door. Both were in the prime of their strength, one broad and muscular, the other as lean as a hairpin.

The thin one had his right hand in his jacket pocket.

It was a nasty moment for the Maggot. He disliked being outnumbered.

'You all right, Edna?'

'I'm fine,' she said. 'This gentleman is just leaving.'

The Maggot glared angrily around him, swung round on his heels and marched out of the shop.

'Thanks guys!' Edna said when he'd gone.

'Edna, that man looks dangerous,' the tall man said to her.

The burly young one was her nephew, who was learning the trade. The other two owned the newsagent's next door. They shared a connecting door upstairs, and they'd fixed up the electric bell so that they could ring each other for help during the blitz.

'I got a lovely pot of vegetable soup going,' Edna said. 'Want to have some later? Come across in about half an hour. And I'll tell you all about it.'

38

Mrs Barnes stood at her kitchen sink feeling happier and more hopeful than she'd felt for ages. Molly and Adam were safely back, her husband was home on leave again, and the War was over – at least, it *would* be if only the Japanese had the sense to surrender.

She heard a movement in the backyard and a shadow fell on the mat by the door.

'Hamish!'

'Hello, Mrs Barnes.'

Mr Barnes came in from the front of the house, wearing a workman's apron and carrying a paintbrush. 'Hamish!' he said, smiling with pleasure. 'I won't shake your hand – I'm covered with paint.'

'Hello, Mr Barnes. What are you painting?'

'Well, we've had our old hallway converted into a reception area, with a proper desk and everything. But I'm doing the decorating myself. How's your summer job?'

Hamish had a holiday job at his uncle's bank in London. He grimaced. 'It's all right, I suppose. But it's not what I want to spend my life doing.'

Then he came to the point. 'Is Molly . . . ?'

'I'm afraid she's gone out,' Mrs Barnes said.

She saw Hamish's face fall and she grieved for him. But when she sensed that her husband was about to give directions to the barn she shook her head at him behind Hamish's back.

'They won't be home till tea-time,' she said. Then, to soften the blow, 'Why don't you wait?'

'But what can I do all afternoon?'

'You can give me a hand if you like,' Molly's dad said.

Hamish brightened. 'I'd like that, sir,' he said. 'Have you an old shirt I could wear?'

They went off together and Mrs Barnes returned to the kitchen sink, pulled out the plug, and thoughtfully rinsed away the washing-up water.

Meanwhile, there was a serpent at Deepney Mere. Not a serpent of sin, but a mean maggoty feeling of restlessness.

Adam swam, read, and sunbathed. He uncovered more of Molly's mediaeval jetty and was good-tempered and cheerful, perfect company in fact. But he would not draw. 'I can't,' he said simply. 'It's gone.'

That wasn't all. Young William had stopped going there with them. 'Want to come?' they'd said. But he shook his head and ran away. It wasn't the same without him. Abigail wasn't the same either. She was restless, impatient, as if her mind was on something else.

The bright August sun cast lopsided shadows that day.

Molly sat with a pad on her bare knees and a pencil in her hand, writing her account of the jetty. Abigail felt restless.

'Molly?'

'Mmm?'

'Hamish – do you *like* him?'

'He's all right. . .'

'*But?*'

'But I wish he wouldn't . . .'

'*I* like him,' Abigail said emphatically. 'A lot.'

'Well, you're welcome to him,' Molly said – and suddenly realised that Abigail had let loose an unnoticed truth. She stared at her in disbelief.

Abigail, standing at the edge of the mere, kicked water all over her.

'*Abigail !* All over my *writing!*'

'It's only a rough copy,' Abigail said – and kicked again. This time Adam got splashed too.

'Right!' he said grimly.

Molly threw aside her work and she and Adam took revenge. Abigail turned to retreat into the mere, but Adam grabbed her and pulled her backwards. Then he took her right leg and right arm, and Molly took her left leg and left arm. Their eyes met over her body, mischievous, cruel. They hauled her into deeper water and threw her in, counting as they swung her – one, two, *three!* And in she went, shrieking.

Late in the afternoon, when Hamish walked through to the back of the house, he found there was more substance in half a dozen words from Molly's mum than in three hours of chat with her dad.

She was in the kitchen. 'Oh, Hamish,' Mrs Barnes said, 'would you help me set the table for tea?'

He took a pile of tea-plates from her hand. 'I hope Molly. . .' he began. He didn't know what he wanted to say.

'Hamish,' Mrs Barnes said. 'It's no use.'

She hadn't intended to say that, or anything like it. The words just came out. His answer was equally direct. 'I know,' he said. 'I knew all along, really.' He put the plates down gently, still in a pile.

Her heart bled for him.

'I don't think I'll stay for tea,' he said. 'I'll get the next train back to town.'

At the door, he turned back. 'You're a jolly decent sort, Mrs Barnes,' he said. 'You're *all* jolly decent!'

39

An unexpected row blew up in Mrs Murfitt's living room, when Ivy had come home from work. She was in a hurry, planning to go out for the evening.

'I'm going to Ely,' she said.

After days of restraint, Abigail unexpectedly challenged her. 'With that man?' she said sharply.

'What man?' Ivy's face, neck and throat flushed. An unmistakable sign of guilt, Molly thought.

'Ivy, who is he?'

'None of your business, *that's* who he is!'

'Ivy, people have seen you! They're talking about you . . . '

'Who do you think you are?' Ivy said. 'Lord, I wish I'd never come to this god-forsaken place! What right have you got, checking up on me like that?'

'Ivy, nobody's checking up on you! But you're *married*.'

That shifted Ivy's anger a little towards wretchedness. 'Yes – and I wish I wasn't!' she muttered.

'You shouldn't be going out with another man.'

'He's just someone I'm going to the pictures with,' Ivy said sulkily. Then she went in for the attack.

'Anyway, what makes you think you can find fault with me? It's because you've *never liked me*!' she shouted. 'Do you think I don't know what you think of me?' She turned her back on them, close to tears. 'You're *snobs*, all three of you! You never wanted me to come here in the first place!'

This was so close to the truth that Molly was startled into feeling ashamed. 'Please, Ivy,' she said. 'It's not like that.'

'So you say! But if it's not true, why do you leave me out of everything? You *never* ask me to do anything with you. You've got this place you go to on hot days – do you think I don't know about it? But you've never once asked me to go too! Not *once*!'

'You wouldn't want to come,' Abigail said.

'You've never given me a chance to find out!'

It was beginning to dawn on Molly that Ivy had successfully turned defence into attack. Then Adam surprised them all. He hardly ever thought about Ivy. As far as he was concerned, she lacked interest. But now she was giving herself some definition.

'I tell you what,' he said mildly. 'Why don't we all go somewhere together – this Saturday when you're not working? The four of us.' He warmed to his idea. 'You choose where you want to go and we'll go together. My treat. Anywhere you like.'

Abigail and Molly were amazed, Ivy suspicious. 'You don't mean it,' she said.

'Yes I do! We'll have a good time. Anywhere you like

– provided I've got enough money. And provided we can get there and back in a day.'

Ivy looked from one to the other, doubtfully, suspiciously. Molly nudged Abigail to agree.

'I'd like to go to London,' Ivy said.

'Where in London?'

'Wait and see!'

'It's true,' Molly said later, 'that we didn't want her to come to the mere. But if she'd been a different kind of person, it wouldn't have mattered.'

'*But*,' Abigail said firmly, 'none of this makes any difference. She's still a married woman going out with another man!'

'Peter, I've been looking around.'

'Dealers?' Mr Fraser asked.

'Yes. And some collectors I know.'

'Found anything?'

'Yes, I have as a matter of fact. There's a lot of crookery in the art world.'

'What have you found?'

Mr Fraser got no reply to that question. 'Peter, can I come and see you?'

'Of course!'

'Today?'

'Yes. Love to see you! Stay the night.'

'Thanks. I'll be starting within the hour.'

40

On Saturday they emerged from Liverpool Street station and took two bus rides and a tram ride, across the river and down into south London. 'I want to see my old house,' Ivy said. 'What's left of it.'

'It's not much of a pleasure trip for you three,' she admitted later. 'But Adam did say I could choose – and this is what I want to do.'

They warmed to her a little. Still, it was a melancholy trip, through miles and miles of unknown streets, all showing the scars of the blitz. They went past a munitions factory. 'That's where I used to work,' Ivy said. Did she want to visit it and see some of her old workmates? No, she said. Anyway, she'd always worked the night-shift and she wouldn't know any of this lot.

They stepped off the bus and Ivy led them towards some shops and a post office. Here they turned into a side street. Ivy stopped and turned white.

Every house had been flattened. On both sides of the road.

Literally *flattened*. Everything had been bulldozed and rolled flat. Usually you saw great craters in the ground, and mountains of fallen masonry. And the surviving buildings would be showing their bare walls, with wallpaper and picture rails and coat hooks. But here there was nothing. Beyond, they could see across the abandoned back gardens that neighbouring streets were exactly the same. All smoothed and levelled. It was weird – this gaunt and tidy desolation.

Two streets away stood a steamroller having a day off.

They were the only people around. *Of course*, Molly thought. *No one lives here any more.*

'Which house was yours?' Abigail asked Ivy.

But Ivy couldn't find it. They moved along the ghost of a street, Ivy growing more and more distressed because she couldn't work out which had been the house where she used to live. 'There was a post-box right outside,' she said. But there were no post-boxes anywhere; no streetlights or telegraph poles either.

She did in the end work out which of the ruins it must have been. They followed her across the door-space, treading on flattened rubble and hard-core, and here they found a few shards of lino that Ivy said came from the kitchen.

Then she started to tremble and shake, and the others concluded it was time they took her away from there. 'Give me a few minutes,' she said. She didn't cry, or go on about it. She just shook from top to toe, clutching her shoulders. 'I couldn't have come here on my own,' she said.

They got her away in the end. They went back towards the shops, and as they were passing the post office a window in the flat upstairs was flung open and a voice screamed, '*Ivy?*'

'*Mrs Percy!*'

The other three stood back while amazed greetings and explanations went on between the street and the upstairs flat. Then Mrs Percy shut the window and came down. 'She runs the post office,' Ivy explained. In what seemed like no time at all, the four of them were ushered into a side door and up the stairs into Mrs Percy's sitting room. Ivy had managed one of her quick recoveries.

'Ivy, m'duck! I never expected to see you no more! Where you bin all this time? Sit down, darlin'. And your friends! Sit down and make yourselves at'ome. *If* you can find a space.'

They were a bit bemused, but they accepted this cheerful invitation.

The room was full of dolls and teddy bears. Mrs Percy saw their surprise and explained. 'They're for company,' she said. 'Since I lost my Rufus.' They didn't ask how she'd lost her Rufus; it was probably her code for a death in the War. She made tea, brought in biscuits and then settled down for a chat.

'You didn't think I'd been killed in the bombing, did you?' Ivy asked.

'No, darlin'. But no one knew where you was! I got this stack of letters for you and I couldn't forward 'em, could I? I asked around but anyone who might have known was killed that day.'

She paused, looking thoughtful. 'Your poor mam!' she said. 'And Mr and Mrs Moorgate who lived next door. *And* their two cats. And do you remember old Dodger Winterbottom? *He* had both legs blown orff and died in the ambulance.'

The list went on as she and Ivy recalled a lost community.

'They're all gorn,' Mrs Percy said. She sniffed and turned to Adam. 'You comfy in that chair?'

'Yes, thank you.'

'That was my Rufus' chair, that was. Best chair in the flat. But would he sit in it? No, he bloody wouldn't! Spent all his time lyin' on the mat with his legs in the air. Mind you, he *did* look lovely! Anyway, ducky. I did try, really I did, to find where you was. I even tried . . .'

She hesitated, then plunged on. 'I even tried your dad.'

'My *dad*?'

'Sorry, ducks. I know you . . . But I thought he might know, see.'

'But he didn't?'

'It's a funny thing. I think he *did* know, but he weren't going to tell no one. He had a funny look on his face when I asked him. You know, shifty like.'

'He always has a shifty look,' Ivy said.

'You know your father?' Molly asked. She tried to remember what she'd been told about Ivy's dad.

'He used to come round sometimes,' Ivy muttered. 'When I was little.'

'Anyway,' Mrs Percy continued, 'there's this pile of mail I got for you.'

'Who's been writing to *me*?' Ivy said. 'No one ever writes to me!'

'Bless you, love, I can tell you who's bin writin' to you! It's the War Office!'

Ivy turned pale. What had she done?

'They got postal orders inside 'em! Once a fortnight they come – payday for servicemen's wives.'

Ivy looked confused.

'You bin and got married to someone, ain't ya? You musta done. Cos every two weeks one of these envelopes arrives, addressed to Mrs Ivy Lea at your old house. It had to be you – no one else lived there except your ole mum.'

'How do you know what's in them? Have you opened them?'

'No! Gawd, I didn't have to open them! I see thousands of 'em! They all look the same. There'll be a postal order in each one.'

'How much?'

'That depends on your hubby's rank.'

'Postal orders?'

'Yes, m' duck. Postal orders. *And* three or four army letters. From overseas.'

Ivy stared. Letters from her husband!

Mrs Percy fetched a bundle of envelopes in a rubber band. 'Yours!' she said triumphantly.

Ivy opened a couple of the WD letters. 'What do I do with these?' she said.

'You cash 'em at a post office.'

'Can I do it here?'

'Course you can't! I'm closed, ain't I? But on Monday you can take them to any post office. Mind you, they probably won't have enough cash in the till to pay it all out in one go. You'll most likely have to spread 'em out over a couple of weeks.'

Ivy's marriage had always had an unreal quality, a phantom incident in someone else's life. But now her husband was solid and substantial. And as soon as the Japanese were defeated he would be on his way home.

And he's never once had a letter from his wife, Molly thought.

41

Letters! No one writes letters any more. It's all emails and text messages now, Molly thinks.

In the toilet, washing her hands in a pink marble washbasin, she feels an acute and familiar need. How long will it take her letter to get to South America? she wonders.

I'm going into hospital shortly for the operation I told you about. It's not especially serious or worrying. But I'd be happier if you were going to be here.

But she'd rewritten it, without the last sentence. She remembers exactly the final version and sometimes repeats it in her head.

Will he come?

Shaking the water from her fingers, she thinks crossly, if he'd use email we could communicate daily! Almost like talking.

Back in the gallery the interviewer leads her to one of the pictures. Cameramen and crew follow. Soft shoes and trailing cables whisper on the wooden floor.

'This image,' the interviewer says, 'keeps appearing in all his work – a young woman standing at an easel. Over and over again. Why did he do that?'

'She was his art teacher's wife,' Molly says.

'Was he in love with her?' the interviewer says. 'After all, he was a fifteen-year-old boy. And she was very beautiful.'

Molly knows it had little to do with adolescent love, or sex. The artist in him wanted to be like that – calmly working, straight-backed and focused.

'Did you mind?'

Molly smiles. 'I suppose I did. A little.'

Marion Fraser was a pillar of loveliness. Adam's eyes were drawn to her all the time, charged with a boy's shameless fascination. Marion understood this, and so did Adam. Neither of them was troubled by it. When he worked close beside her – or when she tucked a scarf around his throat before he cycled home on a cold night – she would smile briefly at him, and he would smile back. Private and conspiratorial, with no mischief in it.

To Molly, she was like a daughter of the gods who had been set down on earth. She was in awe of her, a little jealous.

Marion arrived at the new Deeping Hotel one evening, by herself, in her Austin Seven. 'Is Adam here?' she said.

Everyone crowded into the kitchen – Mrs Barnes, Molly, Abigail, Adam, Ivy, and young William. While the kettle was being boiled, Mrs Fraser explained. 'Mr Royce has found some of your drawings, Adam.'

They braced themselves with anticipation. Mrs Fraser placed on the kitchen table a loosely-wrapped parcel, unfolded it and spread the drawings.

'There are thirty-two here,' she said. 'They *are* yours, aren't they?'

'Where . . . ?'

'Mr Royce found four of them at a dealer's in Piccadilly. He bought them – and then he visited other dealers in search of more.'

'You mean . . . ?' Adam wasn't sure what question he wanted to ask.

'Whoever stole your drawings has sold them to dealers all over London. Mr Royce started to look round – and these are the ones he's found and got back.'

'What about the rest?' Molly asked.

'Well, by questioning the dealers he estimates that about another thirty have already been sold. He found one or two more, bought by people he knows.'

'That leaves some unaccounted for.'

'Yes. He doesn't think we'll be able to trace them all.'

There were many questions, and many explanations. But when their excitement had died down a little, Mrs Fraser said, 'There's another puzzle.'

She picked out one drawing – Molly in her bedroom with the streetlight shining outside her window. 'Mr Royce didn't find this with the others. It was sent to his address. Just this one. There was no letter, and nothing to indicate who'd sent it. Except that it had a London postmark.'

More amazement. *Who* had sent it? *Why* had someone sent it?

'And why this one?'

'It's the best, undoubtedly the best. But why an art thief should choose the single best work and *not* sell it is a mystery.'

'Why would anyone do that?' Ivy said.

Adam picked up the drawing, looked at it briefly and handed it to Molly. William stared quietly, his thumb in his mouth and his body pushed up close to his sister.

Later, Molly sat in the garden with Marion. 'May I ask you something?' she said shyly. Then, without waiting for permission: 'How old were you when you married Mr Fraser?'

Marion smiled. 'Twenty.'

'How old were you when you . . . ?'

'I fell in love with him when I was seventeen – and he was fifty. And I've never regretted it for a moment! He was my tutor at college – a *brilliant* teacher, kind, patient, inspirational.'

She turned towards Molly. 'May I say something to you?'

Molly nodded, wonderingly.

'Artists can be very –' she sought the right word '– *consuming*,' she said. 'They can be greedy. If you're close to one, you can easily get overwhelmed.'

'I know,' Molly said. She'd thought about this. 'Did that happen to you?'

'No,' Marion said thoughtfully. 'I've always taken care that he should *not* be overwhelmed. And fortunately he is a very independent person.'

Molly was flummoxed. She spent some moments framing a question which would clear things up without revealing her confusion. 'When I've been to your studio,' she said cautiously, 'I've noticed that there is not much of *your* work displayed there.'

'That's because I send it off to London as soon as I'm satisfied with it. To be sold, or exhibited.'

Molly stared. 'Oh.'

'Paterson Royce sells most of it. He's a very good dealer. Even during the War he managed to find buyers.'

Why didn't Adam tell *me?* Molly thought furiously.

As they slept that night, the sun rose on the far side of the world. Small people in a big Japanese city gazed up in mild puzzlement at a falling parachute. They were accustomed to US reconnaissance planes passing over their city. But the parachute – what did that mean?

The B29 headed away. The parachute, tiny in the immense dawn sky, fell steadily earthward.

A woman outside her street door stooped over her flowerpots with a watering can; a naked baby boy waved his feet in the air as he waited for his mother to dress him; two little girls walked hand-in-hand to school; an old man in a temple garden carefully raked his gravel into patterns of tranquillity.

From horizon to horizon, there was a blinding magnesium flash, like a new sun filling the entire sky.

Did they feel an instant of dismay, of terror? Did they experience a pain beyond all imagining? Or were they annihilated at once, in a timeless moment, along with the other sixty or seventy thousand?

Prompt and utter annihilation, as promised.

42

Sometimes things happen without apparent cause. There's no understanding why an event which happens one day hadn't happened the day before, or several days before; or several days later. Or not at all. Out of the blue it comes, like a thunderstroke.

In Mrs Barnes' kitchen one afternoon they heard a voice.

It was strange – a voice that spoke as if they were perfectly familiar with it. And yet they'd never heard it before. There was something *faerie* about it, as if a chair had spoken, or the teapot.

Of *course* it was strange to them! Because a five-year-old silence had turned itself into speech. Perfect sentences, perfectly expressed. Just as the doctor had predicted.

'Ivy took Adam's drawings,' William said. 'She put them in an envelope. It was a very big envelope. Like a parcel. Then she went out with it.'

It was the others who were speechless then – stunned partly by the news itself, but also by their realisation that the wrong reply might silence the speaker for another five years. Or the rest of his life.

Molly settled it. 'Did you see her?'

William nodded, but he looked surprised for a moment, taken aback. 'Yes, I was there,' he said. 'I saw her . . . '

He seemed not to be self-conscious at all. As if, Molly thought afterwards, he'd been saying things inside his head for years and was perfectly used to it. And *that* was why he'd looked surprised – of all the thousands of things he'd said in the quiet of his mind, this was the first time anyone had answered him.

43

There was something helpless about Frosty. There he was, buying a ticket at Liverpool Street station – and he hadn't the faintest idea that he was under observation!

Not the faintest! Yet Jimmy Riddle stood right behind him.

Jimmy ducked his head and turned aside as Frosty left the queue. 'Same again,' he said to the ticket clerk. With his own ticket, he followed Frosty at a distance and boarded the train in a different carriage. Only then did he inspect his ticket. Ely? Where's *that*? he thought.

At Ely, Frosty didn't even look behind him. He walked out of the station and into the town, up the hill and into the market-place. He never once looked back, not once.

In the middle of town there was a café close to the cinema. Frosty peered through the window and waved briefly to someone inside. Jimmy Riddle stayed in the street, keeping an eye on the door of the café. Later, Frosty came out with a young woman, a bit of a looker, Jimmy thought. The two of them, absorbed in one another, crossed the road to the cinema and went in.

Jimmy dutifully entered the cinema and bought himself a ticket. When his eyes had accustomed themselves to the darkness he found Frosty and his friend sitting a few rows in front. This was convenient because he could keep them in view. But they just sat there, watching the film, occasionally exchanging a whispered word or two, and sharing a packet of sweets. Holding hands too, probably, but he couldn't see that.

I want to know if anyone gives him anything. Anything at all! Those were Jimmy's instructions. But in the darkness of the cinema how could he see what was going on?

It was almost dark when they came out. Jimmy followed the two of them back to the railway station. There was a long goodbye hug. She was a pretty girl. (*Lucky blighter!* Jimmy thought). Then she got on a train going in the other direction and Frosty set off down the tunnel to cross to the opposite platform for the London train.

Jimmy was feeling depressed. He didn't like this kind of job and, besides, Frosty was one of his mates. For two pins he'd just go straight home. Or he could even warn Frosty. Someone ought to. Then the matter was settled for him. The tunnel was curved like the end of a paper clip, and as Frosty turned into the second curve he looked back and saw his follower coming round the first one.

His step faltered, he stopped. 'Jimmy? Is that you? What the hell are you doing here?'

Jimmy Riddle sighed and thought *that's another job*

244

I've messed up! 'Hello, Frosty,' he said. 'It's a long story, mate.'

Slowly they walked up the slope to platform two. 'I've been tailing you, Frosty, that's what.'

'The Maggot?' You could hear the fear in his voice.

'Yeah. Listen, Frosty. He's really got it in for you, mate! Ever since you started selling on your own. That's why I'm s'posed to be tailin' you. He wants to know where you're getting your supplies.'

Frosty glumly protested. 'But I've got rid of it all – there ain't no more.'

'Try telling *him* that! Remember what happened to Willy Wilson?'

Frosty stared. 'You don't mean . . .? *Me*?'

'You're in big trouble, mate. You need to be *very* careful. I don't mind tellin' you, he scares the life out of me, with those mean little eyes – and that nasty little secret up his sleeve.'

'All I did was sell some stuff to someone else!'

'Frosty, do you carry anything?'

'What d'you mean?'

'A gun? A knife?'

Frosty whispered his appalled reply. '*No!* I ain't never had neither.'

'He hates you, Frosty.'

It had never occurred to Frosty that he was important enough to be hated. 'What am I going to do?'

The London train arrived and they found seats

together, the follower and the followed, facing each other, leaning forward, knee to knee.

'If I were you, I'd get out of London. Straightaway!'

But Frosty had never lived anywhere else. He'd hardly ever *been* anywhere else.

'There's other places, mate. Manchester, Newcastle, Glasgow.' As far as Frosty was concerned, he might just as well have suggested Hong Kong or Shanghai.

'You can get out of this, Frosty, you *can*! Start a new life somewhere. Marry that bird and take her with you.'

'*Marry* her?' Frosty said. 'I don't want to . . . Anyway, she's already married.'

Oh, it's like that, is it, Jimmy Riddle thought to himself.

At Liverpool Street, Jimmy found a public telephone and called the Maggot. *Yes, Frosty did meet someone. A woman, and they went to the pictures. No, Frosty wasn't carrying no packages afterwards. He just said goodbye to the bird and got a train back to London.*

44

Mr and Mrs Fraser visited again. Paterson Royce, they said, had managed to trace another fifteen of Adam's drawings. The others were in the hands of private collectors. Still, in total, Adam had got back about half the missing artwork.

Mr Fraser said: 'Paterson Royce has a proposition.'

Very clearly, young William said, 'What's a proposition?'

'He's having an exhibition in the autumn and he wants to include some of your work, Adam.'

'An exhibition of Adam's drawings?' Molly said.

'No. There will be several artists, but Adam will be one of them. He wants to include about ten of Adam's pieces.'

They could see Mr Fraser's pride in his young pupil's success. Mrs Barnes was proud too; she went round the table and hugged Adam.

'They would be for sale,' Mr Fraser continued, 'and he would take a commission. And the exhibits must include the *Streetlight* drawing.'

Adam said: 'He's welcome to exhibit it, but he can't sell it.'

'Why not?'

'It isn't mine to sell. It belongs to Molly.'

Molly was wide-eyed. That was the first she knew that the drawing was hers.

In her quiet and authoritative voice, Marion said, 'You mustn't always give your work to your sitter, Adam.'

'It's Molly's,' Adam said firmly. 'She can sell it if she likes.'

Never! thought Molly.

Then the Frasers raised another difficult issue – the police. 'Paterson thinks – and I think so too –' Mr Fraser said, 'that he should now report this whole matter to Scotland Yard.'

Adam was emphatic. 'No,' he said.

'Adam,' Marion said, 'this is a serious case of art theft. And your drawings were sold as Picassos, which makes it a complicated case of fraud as well. You can't just ignore it.'

'Yes I can,' Adam said.

There was no changing his mind.

He may not be doing any drawing at the moment, Molly's mum thought, but he *is* his old self again – ungainsayable.

The factory where Ivy worked closed down for a week in August. And Ivy had gone to stay in Yarmouth for a few days with some of her workmates. That was why she wasn't there when young William told everyone what she'd done.

But now she was back, bouncy and cheerful, and bright as a button. She'd had a *marvellous* time, she said. Yarmouth wasn't as good as Brighton, but still . . . there were young men all over the place! Newly demobbed, looking for fun.

The others were stern and unimpressed. 'Ivy?' Abigail said.

'What now?'

Abigail went straight to the point. 'Who stole Adam's drawings?'

'How should I know?'

'Did *you* take them?'

'No!'

Abigail's approach lacked subtlety. 'We think you did,' she said.

The tilt of Ivy's chin went up a little. 'Who says I did?'

'William,' Abigail said. 'William says he saw you take them.'

Ivy was contemptuous. '*William?* He never says anything! Everyone knows he's touched in the head!'

The brutishness of Ivy's words outraged Molly. She stepped forward and slapped the side of Ivy's face. Then she turned her back on all of them.

Abigail was brutal and accusing. Ivy was her relative and she felt shamed by her. 'William saw you take the drawings and put them in a parcel. Now they've begun to turn up for sale all over London.'

Ivy stared, her left hand pressed against her cheek. 'It wasn't me.'

'Prove it!' Abigail snapped.

'It's not up to me to prove it,' Ivy said. 'I didn't do it and you can't prove I did!'

'William says you did.'

'It's just my word against . . . against a little kid's,' she said.

'There have been investigations,' Abigail continued. 'About half of the drawings have been recovered.'

'What do you mean?' This was Ivy's lowest point.

'I mean that we have them back.'

'I don't believe you.'

'We have around fifty of them,' Adam said. He felt detached from this questioning of Ivy. He kept looking out of the window – at the world outside, where Mrs Murfitt was peaceably hoeing in her vegetable garden.

It was Abigail's choice of words that had done for Ivy. *Investigations* suggested the police. So did the words *have been recovered*. To Ivy, language like that was almost as powerful as evidence. She caved in at once.

'So what if I did? You had no right to hit me, Molly Barnes!'

'I had every right,' Molly snapped back. 'You're a *thief*, Ivy.' Though that wasn't why she'd hit her.

'I didn't do it for myself,' Ivy said.

The talk lost all sense at this stage, with everyone

speaking at once. They moved about the room, interrupted, reproached, threatened, comforted one another, failed to listen to what was said. It went on and on, getting nowhere, until Adam said, 'How did you get the pictures to all those galleries?'

There was a sudden hush.

'I didn't,' Ivy said. 'I sent them to my dad.'

'Your *dad*? But you don't know your dad!'

'Who says I don't know him? Course I know him. I've always known him!'

'But your mum . . .'

'My mum couldn't stand him! She wouldn't have him in the house. But I saw him a lot. Always did! So there!'

Adam wasn't interested in Ivy's complicated family pattern. He wanted to know about his drawings. 'Why did you give them to your father?'

'He *deals* in things. That's what he *does*!'

'You mean he's a spiv,' Abigail snapped. 'I suppose he sells stolen goods and black market stuff.'

'Call him what you like,' Ivy said. 'He's been called names all his life! That's the *point*! I thought he deserved a bit of good luck for a change. So when I saw all them drawings . . .'

'You stole them and gave them to him to sell.'

'Yes,' Ivy said defiantly. 'And he made a lot of money on them too!' It didn't seem to occur to her that this did not make the theft less serious; or that her dad might now have to pay the money back.

All this was too much for Molly. 'But they weren't his to sell,' she said unhappily. 'They were Adam's – and you just helped yourself to them and gave them to your rotten father to get rid of.'

Rotten father was the trigger this time. 'Don't you talk to me about fathers, any of you!' Ivy shouted. 'You don't know what it's like to have a decent dad! I *love* my dad, even though everyone treats him like shit! He's always been good to me.'

'What do you mean, *we don't know what it's like to have a decent dad*?'

'Well, look at you,' Ivy said to Molly. 'You want to go to college – but your dad doesn't care what *you* want. *He* just wants you to be a skivvy in his fancy hotel! Working for nothing, probably. So don't you talk to me about fathers! You don't know what it's like to have one who cares about you.'

'It's not true,' Molly said. 'He's changed his mind about that. I can go to university if I want to. He *said*.'

Ivy sneered. 'Only cos he wants you to be like Mister Lah-de-Dah Hamish! It's not because he cares about what *you* want!'

Ivy was needle-sharp, and Molly was silenced.

Ivy hadn't finished. She turned to Abigail. 'And your dad's no better. He loves you so much that he can't wait to get away! Every other soldier wants to get home with his family – but no sooner is your dad demobbed than he's signed on again! He'd rather be in Berlin than here.

So don't you talk to me about fathers, Abigail Murfitt! You might as well not have one!'

Ivy paused, but only to draw breath. She turned to Adam. 'And *your* father's so keen on *you* that he's arranged for you to live eighty miles from home!'

'Have you finished now?' Adam said.

'No! As a matter of fact, I haven't. You *hate* me, all of you. You always did, from the day I got here. And people feel the same about my ole dad.'

'Ivy . . .'

'So we stick together, see? He looks out for me, and I look out for him.' She paused. 'And if I have to go to prison, it'll be better than this rotten place. Nobody's been nice to me here, *nobody*!'

But her fury seemed to be exhausting itself. Adam, unruffled and mildly puzzled, said, 'One of the stolen drawings was sent directly to a dealer? Why did your dad do that?'

'He didn't. That was me.'

'Why?'

Ivy scowled and fidgeted. 'Because I thought if someone important saw it they might make you famous. I was doing you a *favour*!'

'But how did you know where to send it?'

'There was a card with the bloke's address on it. In your folder.'

'But why *that* drawing?'

'Well, it was the best. Anyone could see that!'

'Oh, *Ivy*!' Molly said.

'What happens now?' Ivy said. She was subdued, worn out. 'The police, I s'pose.'

'No,' Adam said. 'Not the police.' He understood the complicated distress that would be caused if Ivy's crime were exposed.

Molly stared at him. Abigail looked as if she was about to protest. But they both knew that look on Adam's face.

'Will you tell your mum? ' Ivy said to Abigail.

Abigail was confused. 'I don't know,' she snapped. 'Probably not. But Molly's mum already knows, and they're best friends.'

Ivy brightened up. 'Oh, well then,' she said cheerfully. 'I'm going to have a bath, if you haven't used up all the hot water, Abigail Murfitt!'

She was amazing. Extraordinary! She slipped comfortably back into normal life as if nothing much had happened. *If I'd been found out in a theft like that,* Molly thought, *I'd be so humiliated that nothing could ever be the same again. Yet* she *just goes off to have a bath!*

'She's full of surprises, our Ivy,' Abigail muttered when Ivy left the room.

As for Adam, he went into town and found a crowd of boys playing football against the wall of the gasworks. He joined in and they played for hours – until it was too dark to see the ball.

45

Lots of men look like thugs, with thick necks, blunt heads and expressionless faces. Yet most of them will be perfectly nice men, kind and thoughtful. However, some men who look like thugs actually *are* thugs. That must happen sometimes, stands to reason.

The Maggot had two men like that. And when Jimmy Riddle got a summons to meet him and his two henchmen, his heart sank. One of them was called Big Ben, the other Thatch (probably because he was as bald as an egg). They scared him just by existing. They had no families; they had no mates; they had no interest in football. Their eyes were dead and, if you tried to start a conversation, you just got a grunt and a blank look.

But the Maggot found they came in useful.

'Where we going?' Jimmy asked.

'We're going to pay Frosty a visit,' the Maggot said.

Frosty lived at number seven, Mafeking Road; a tall Victorian terraced house.

'Trust him to live at the top,' the Maggot grumbled as they toiled up the staircase. It was shabby, this old house; but at least it was still standing. At the other end of the road they'd all been blitzed. Years ago, in 1940.

There was no reply when they knocked. A woman's voice yelled up from the ground floor. 'He ain't in!'

The Maggot leaned over the banister and shouted down the stair-well. 'Do you know when he'll be back?'

'No, I don't.'

'Are you the landlady?'

'No, I ain't.'

'D'you know where he's gorn?'

'No, I don't.'

'Will you . . . ?'

A door was slammed shut. *No, she wouldn't.*

One of the thugs gave the Maggot a *shall-we?* look. But he shook his head and nodded at Jimmy Riddle. So Jimmy got out his bunch of skeleton keys and knelt down at the keyhole. It was so pitifully easy a child could've picked this lock with a hairpin! Jimmy stood up and opened the door.

Inside it was quiet and empty. There were two rooms: a small kitchen and a large bed-sitting room. It was clean and tidy too. Quite comfortable, in fact, and from the windows there were good views of the surrounding bombsites.

'He's done a bunk,' Jimmy said. He said it as if he was outraged.

The Maggot was looking down at the doormat. 'There ain't no letters,' he said. 'Which means someone has forwarded his mail – which means that someone knows his address.'

Proper Sherlock Holmes, Jimmy thought. 'There ain't

no letterbox neither,' he said – and got an angry glare from the Maggot.

The Maggot went through every drawer and cupboard. He looked behind the wireless and under the mat, everywhere. But all he could find were clothes, toothpaste, cleaning powder. Exactly what you'd find in a million other households.

'Boss,' Jimmy said nervously. 'Why does it matter?'

The Maggot banged his fist down on the table with such ferocity that even the two thugs were startled. 'Because Frosty is doing me down! Do you know how? You don't, do you? I'll tell you.'

He didn't shout. His voice was low, a gravelly growl. 'He's found a supplier and he's selling stuff on his own. And d'you know what he's selling? Pictures! Bloody pictures! He's flogging them all over London and he's making *thousands*! Thousands of pounds!'

Jimmy doubted it. He could imagine Frosty dealing in a lorry-load of copper pipes, or ex-army uniforms. But *pictures*? Never! 'Where's he getting them from?' he asked.

'That's what I want to know,' the Maggot said. 'Frosty could make a *fortune* out of this!' His eye fell on a framed photo of a young woman, which stood on a chest of drawers. 'Is that the bird you saw him with?'

Jimmy studied the photo. 'It might be. But I never got a close look at her. She's a good-looking bit of stuff.'

'I want her found,' the Maggot said slowly to Jimmy. 'Understand?'

Jimmy had no idea how he could find this young woman. 'I don't think she has anything to do with it,' he said.

'Maybe not. But she probably knows where he's gorn. Or she might have scarpered with him. Nobody screws me! *Nobody!* And we all know what happens to people who try.'

46

When Jimmy Riddle had advised him to go into hiding, Frosty had left the train at Cambridge and found himself a place. On his third day there he phoned Jimmy Riddle at *The Greyhound* in Hackney, where he liked to play backgammon with a group of his mates.

'Jimmy, will you do me a favour?'

'What?' Jimmy was cautious by nature.

'Will you get something from my flat and post it to me?'

'Your flat?' Jimmy didn't tell Frosty that he'd just been there, with the Maggot.

'Yeah. There's a photograph . . .'

'A photograph!'

'Come on, Jimmy. It means a lot to me, that picture.'

Jimmy was thinking it through. A morning – that's how long it would take. Well, why not?

'How will I know which picture to get?'

'Cos there's only one.'

'I haven't got a key.'

'Come off it! *You* wouldn't need a key to get inside the Bank of England!'

'OK. But I need your address so that I can send

it. Hold on – I got to find a pencil.'

'It's Flat 13, Kite Mansions, Cambridge.'

'Right, mate! Got it!'

So next morning Jimmy Riddle went into south London and made his way to the house where Frosty had his apartment. The house was quiet, not a soul to be seen in the hall or on the stairs.

Jimmy reached the top floor and pick-locked the door faster than most people could do it with a key. Inside, he stood still and looked carefully around him. This was second nature to him – entering unfamiliar rooms, then silently waiting to see if there was anything dangerous.

He'd trained himself as an observer over the years and on the previous visit he'd memorised every detail. Nothing had been moved, he was sure of that.

And yet he felt uneasy.

Still, the picture was barely two paces away, on the table. But the photo was in a heavy frame which would be a nuisance to wrap up in a package. So Jimmy undid the clips at the back, and took the picture out.

Something was written on the photo, along the bottom, unseen at first because it was hidden by the frame. *With all my love, Ivy. X*

Suddenly Jimmy froze. Something – certainly not his sense of sight – told him that this was a big mistake. *Hearing* then? No! It was a *smell*! Why hadn't he noticed it before? The apartment smelt of soap – to be precise, shaving soap.

The door to the kitchen had been silently opened and there stood Big Ben, wearing only his underpants, and with his face half-shaved.

If Frosty shows up, the Maggot had said, *smash 'im up. If it's Jimmy, smash him up, cos I don't trust him neither.*

Big Ben didn't ask questions. That's not what thugs do. Nor did he tease, or mock. But he did smile, just a little and Jimmy had a couple of seconds to anticipate the pain. Then it arrived – a grinding mix of sound, sensation, and smell. The sound was of his teeth, crunching in his mouth. The sensation was of his entire face smashed. And the smell was the dusty floorboards into which his head was trodden violently down by a bare foot – big, and none too clean.

Jimmy passed out. When he came to, he was alone. He could hear footsteps going down the stairs to the hall. *Well, I'm alive. I suppose that's something,* Jimmy thought. Then, *Sod you, Frosty! I should've kept well out of your business!*

When he tried to sit up, he felt the aches and bruises all over his body. And it was hard to draw breath. There was a tooth jammed between two floorboards, with blood on it. But it was his face that worried him. He had an image in his mind of a lump of meat with no features.

He dragged himself to his feet and made his way to a mirror. And in the middle of all that pain he had a moment of genuine thankfulness, almost joy – at the discovery that *he still had his face*. There was a massive injury to his right forehead, and a huge bruise was already swelling up around one eye. His lips were swollen and cut. And his tongue, feeling around inside his mouth, found that some long-familiar landmarks had changed. But he still had his face.

Then he was sick. Painfully and violently into Frosty's lav.

Jimmy had a sister who lived in Barnet. Ever since he was a kid, he'd always gone to her when he was in trouble. She had a lovely little back bedroom and she never asked no questions.

But Barnet was a hell of a long way off! Right at the top end of London.

He checked his possessions. His money was still there. So was his wallet. But what *had* gone was the bit of paper with Frosty's address on it: *Frosty – Flat 13, Kite Mansions, Cambridge*. And the photo, that had gone too.

Poor ole Frosty! They'll kill him, no doubt about it.

Jimmy didn't know how he managed to get down the stairs. He was dizzy and couldn't walk straight. He staggered against the wall and clung to the banister. At one point he gave up, sat down and lowered his behind slowly from one step to the next.

Out in the street he crashed sideways into a passer-by. 'Here! You all right, mate?'

'A post office,' Jimmy said. He *felt* as if blood and spit bubbled out of his mouth as he spoke, but it didn't. Not much anyway. 'Is there a post office?'

'You need an orspital, tha's what you need!'

'Please.'

'Just round the corner. Here, I'll give you an 'and.'

People get medals for being heroic. And so they should. But you only get a medal if you're *seen* doing something brave. Every day, thousands of people do heroic things that no one knows anything about.

Jimmy Riddle should have got a medal for what it cost him – in pain, effort, concentration – to go into a post office, remember Frosty's address and dictate a telegram message, when he could've been on his way to his sister's.

Half an hour later, with his poor hurt head leaning against the window on a northbound tram, Jimmy allowed himself to think about his sister's lovely back bedroom – where the narrow bed was pushed up against the radiator, and where you could hear women talking as they hung out their washing, and Enid moving about in the kitchen downstairs.

47

An hour or two later, in Cambridge, there was a knock on Frosty's door. Frosty had been asleep in an armchair. He awoke, startled – then scared. Who could be knocking on his door? No one knew where he was!

He waited, in case whoever it was went away. But they didn't, and there was another knock. But this time someone called out. 'Anyone at home? There's a telegram.'

A *telegram*? Frosty never had telegrams! Telegrams happened to people who had sons or husbands in the War. He opened the door, fearing a trick. But there was no trick – just a telegraph boy, looking anxious. 'You have to sign,' he said.

Frosty closed the door and opened the telegram. GET OUT NOW REPEAT NOW J.

Frosty didn't waste time working out what had gone wrong. The message was clear. It took barely three minutes to stuff his possessions into the small suitcase he'd bought on Cambridge market.

As he packed, his mind was working out what he should do. He must leave Cambridge, that was clear. But not by train. If he went to the railway station he'd probably meet the Maggot and his henchmen. But he'd been in Cambridge long enough to find his way about. And he knew where the buses started. Wherever he went, it would have to be by bus.

He opened the door and stepped cautiously onto the dusty carpeted corridor. There was not a sound. Frosty hurried downstairs and out into the street, half-expecting at any minute to be pulled into a dark corner, or to meet head-on with a fist like a bag of cement.

But that didn't happen. He got safely to Drummer Street and found the right bus.

Hamish sat eating his lunchtime sandwiches in the dappled warmth of a London garden square. He felt low-spirited and he wished bitterly that he had not said such a final goodbye to the people at Great Deeping.

He missed them. *All* of them. Not just Molly, not especially Molly if he was honest. He thought Mrs Barnes was perfect. Adam was OK too. And Abigail Murfitt was a jolly good sport.

But what could he do? As far as Deeping went, he'd burnt his boats. But maturing schoolboys have ways of bringing about what they want. He jumped to his feet and set off for the nearest Underground station.

It was hot and stuffy at Liverpool Street station but Hamish felt buoyant, full of purpose. The train would get him to Great Deeping late in the afternoon – and his plan was to invite his friends to a supper at the local fish and chip café. It would be his treat, and would cover all embarrassment. Then he'd get the last train back.

At Cambridge three men entered his compartment. Two sat opposite him, one beside him. After a while the oldest of the three said, 'Let's have another dekko at that picture.'

One of the others took a creased and folded photograph from his inside pocket and passed it across. The older man opened it out and all three leaned forward to study it.

It was a photo of a young woman, and Hamish was taken aback to find that he recognised her. It was Abigail's cousin! He was sure! He hardly knew her, but he'd seen her a few times. It *was* her. *Ivy*, her name was. There was handwriting, too. *With all my love, Ivy.* That settled it.

And when the older man turned the picture over, Hamish saw there was a label on the back: *Crowther's Photographic Studio, Ely*. There was an identical label on the back of all his school photos. And someone had written *Railway Cottage, King George Street, Gt. Deeping*.

It was Abigail's address.

Hamish studied the passing countryside, impassive, every inch an unruffled young gentleman from a public school. But his mind was in a fever. What could these three men want with Ivy?

One of the bigger men said, 'Suppose he ain't there, boss?' and the older one answered, 'Then we'll *wait*!'

That was all. But Hamish was sure that someone (male) was expected to come in search of Ivy and these three were intent on making contact with him. Then a reckoning would be settled.

Earlier, he had been unable to decide whether he would go first to Molly's house, or to Abigail's. But now it was clear that he must get to Railway Cottage first – and warn Ivy.

48

At Great Deeping that afternoon the air was hot and sultry. People were plagued by millions of thunder-midges. They didn't bite or sting – but they found their way into nostrils and ears, inside clothing, in people's hair. And they penetrated picture frames and made tiny changes to the pictures.

Molly, Abigail and Adam had spent the afternoon swimming at the mere. It was the best place to be on a day like that. At around tea time the girls went to Abigail's house and Adam did some shopping for Mrs Barnes.

In the oppressive silence a bell clattered to signal the approach of the down train from London. Abigail shouted, 'I'll do it!' She closed both gates to traffic, and then went to the small sentry-box to pull the lever which set the train-signal to *GO*. Mechanical locking ensured that she couldn't do this unless the gates were first closed to road traffic. So, although Abigail was under-age and therefore illegal, she couldn't get it wrong.

As she waited, she wiped her sweaty face. It felt as if her hair was full of midges. A faint rumble of thunder came from thirty miles away. Despite the heat, Abigail shivered and there were goosepimples along her arms.

She felt the huge metallic heat of the locomotive as the train thundered slowly by, reducing speed. When it had passed, Abigail set the signal to *STOP* and opened the gates. A tractor and a butcher's van crossed the tracks – and a woman with a pram, wiping the sweat from her brow with one arm and clumsily pushing with the other.

Back in her garden, Abigail found Molly staring into the road. 'What is it?'

'Another Lurker,' Molly said quietly.

Abigail stared. A stranger stood in the road. He looked hot and worried.

He carried an overcoat and a small suitcase. 'Perhaps he's looking for the station,' Abigail said – and she was about to go to the garden gate and give him directions.

But it was Abigail's house he was studying – and he kept looking back along the street. 'I told you,' Molly whispered. 'He's *lurking*.'

At that moment Ivy came into view, coming home from work. Their hearts hardened at the sight of her. Then, to their surprise, she started to run towards the Lurker. Then he turned and saw her. Ivy fell into his arms and they held each other. They could see Ivy's rapturous face as it snuggled into the side of the big man's neck.

'So *that's* who he is!'

Mrs Murfitt had come along beside them. 'Mum,' Abigail said recklessly. 'Ivy's got a boyfriend!'

Mrs Murfitt stared for a moment or two. 'That's not Ivy's boyfriend,' she said. 'That's her father.'

'She's full of surprises, our Ivy,' Abigail said softly.

'This is my dad,' Ivy called out. 'Come on, you two, come and meet my dad!'

But Mrs Murfitt turned and went inside, just as Abigail saw Hamish racing along Green Lane towards them. 'Hamish!' she cried. 'What on earth . . . ?'

Hamish staggered up to them, hot-faced. He bent down, gasping for breath, with his hands on his knees, then dropped his jacket and tie on the ground. His hair was spiky where he'd wiped the sweat from his face.

He straightened up and gasped, 'Who's this?'

Such abruptness was not characteristic. Nor was his dishevelled appearance.

'This is my dad,' Ivy said. (*She keeps saying that*, Molly thought irritably.)

'Ah!' Hamish said, still breathless. 'I think you might be in some danger, sir.'

Ivy and Frosty glanced nervously at each other. Molly and Abigail just looked bewildered. 'Why?'

'There are three men coming here. They're looking for someone.'

'But what makes you think . . .?'

Hamish tried to keep his explanation short and precise. 'They were on the train. And they had a photo of Ivy. This address was written on the back of it, and this is where they're coming. I think they mean you harm, sir.'

There were lots of buts and ifs from Molly and Abigail, but Frosty just said, 'A small older man and two big ones?'

'Yes.'

Poor Frosty felt his heart sinking to his boots. 'What are we going to do?' Ivy said, clutching his arm anxiously.

'I have to get away,' Frosty said. 'And I can't ever go back to London. Not any more.'

'But why . . ? Why do these men . . ?'

Hamish interrupted. 'I don't think there's time for a discussion,' he said politely. 'They're on their way – now. Ivy's father needs somewhere to hide.'

'The barn!' Molly said. Abigail agreed at once. 'Yes, I'll take them! But –' she said to Molly, '– you should go and find Adam.'

The sky was as dark as night-time, though it was only six o' clock. As Molly raced through the gloom, she saw three men approaching from the station. One of them – a huge burly figure – was clutching his head and stooping as he walked.

There was a rumble of thunder, closer than before. The big man almost collapsed, terrified.

49

On their way to the Barn, Abigail hurriedly explained to Hamish about the sale of Adam's drawings. 'What an absolute bounder!' Hamish muttered.

Inside the barn, Ivy stood with her hand nervously clutching Frosty's arm. They looked scared and uneasy. It was a strange, un-London-like building. A lurid light came through square unglazed windows high in the walls and through the half-open door.

Abigail hoped they wouldn't notice the staircase to their secret room. That was private, sacrosanct. Luckily a huge old threshing-machine – dusty, cobwebby, covered in flaking pink paint – hid the staircase from view. *But if we hide up there,* she thought, *they'll search. And they'll find it.*

The lightning was more frequent now, and the thunder louder.

There was an embarrassed silence – what could they possibly talk about?

'Mr Winters,' said Abigail (she *had* to say something), 'Have you still got some of Adam's drawings?'

Frosty shook his head and cleared his throat.

'They've all gone,' he said. His voice sounded as if

it came from some deep bubbly place in his chest.

Three figures appeared silently in the doorway, then entered the Barn. The Maggot peered this way and that, searching. A smile flickered on his face when he saw Frosty. He ignored Hamish and Abigail; they were of no significance.

Frosty sighed deeply.

Big Ben was in big trouble. He could hardly stand, and he looked terrified. 'I hate thunderstorms,' he said. At that moment there was a loud crash of thunder, close overhead. He wailed pathetically and pressed himself into a corner, half hiding behind an old wooden tailboard that leaned against the wall.

The Maggot approached Frosty. Abigail reached her hand towards Ivy, inviting her away, but Ivy wouldn't leave her dad.

'Nice to see you, Frosty,' growled the Maggot.

'What are you doing here?' Frosty said.

'Oh, I think you know what I'm here for, Frosty,' the Maggot said gently. 'Listen, darlin', you might not want to see what's going to happen to your boyfriend, know what I mean?' He was speaking to Ivy but he never took his eyes off Frosty.

'I'm not her boyfriend,' Frosty said.

Ivy said nothing. She seemed mesmerised.

'And you two,' the Maggot snapped, 'piss off out of here!'

'You do know you're trespassing?' Hamish said.

It was a feeble protest and the Maggot ignored it.

'How much did you make, Frosty? Hundreds of pounds, was it? Or *thousands*?'

At that moment there was a fierce quivering flash of lightning and simultaneously a colossal explosion of thunder immediately overhead. Adam and Molly slipped into the doorway of the barn, unnoticed because everyone else – even the Maggot – at that moment had looked instinctively up at the roof.

Big Ben began to whimper in terror. Adam pulled Molly into the shadow of a tractor.

'Since your friends insist on staying,' the Maggot said slowly, 'I think you'd better introduce me, Frosty.'

'This is – this is Mr Maggs,' Frosty said. 'He taught me all I know.'

Was Frosty trying to be funny? Mr Maggs chuckled pleasantly. 'Not *all* I know, Frosty, mate. Cos I'm going to teach you one more lesson.' He slipped his right hand across to his left sleeve and a knife appeared in it. Its blade shone in the gloom.

That was when Molly understood that when big things happen – tragic things, or heroic things, or violent unspeakable things – they aren't accompanied by rising background music. They grow unnoticed out of ordinary living; they slip sideways into ordinary time; they even have their own ordinariness.

Thatch looked worried. 'Boss, you said just . . .'

'Shut up, Thatch!'

'But there's all these witnesses!'

'Witnesses ain't never bothered me before.' The

Maggot spoke, low and confident. 'Do you know one of the things I've always hated about you, Frosty? You're *taller* than me – and I don't like that.' Then, suddenly savage and sharp, 'So get down on your knees.'

Frosty shook his head. Was he paralysed with terror? Was he perhaps trying to show some dignity, some defiance, in front of his daughter?

'I *said* . . .'

Adam stood motionless in the shadows, attentive, understanding the situation. There was no longer any possibility of visiting his rage on Frosty. There wasn't enough substance in Frosty to be angry with. Frosty was the victim now – and this was a different kind of wickedness. Adam saw clearly into the very heart of the Maggot's cold and deliberate malice.

Then the rain arrived, a relentless deafening downpour, hissing, roaring. It had swept across the Fens, a wall of water. Several billion thunder-midges were downed in the first instant, or smashed to death in the second.

'Boss,' Thatch said uneasily, 'there's all these others!' But the Maggot was savage beyond all caring.

A violent crash of thunder exploded immediately over the roof. There was a flash of flame and the cracking sound of something being torn apart. The oak tree outside split in two and burst briefly into flame. This was too much for Big Ben. He collapsed to the floor and covered his head with his arms. He pressed against the wall and rocked backwards and forwards, moaning.

Everyone was distracted briefly. When they turned back to the main action there was blood on the side of Frosty's face, little dark beads bubbling out from a shallow cut. It was a perfect arc from brow to chin, as if an artist had drawn it there, in dark-red ink. Frosty stood motionless, in despair. Ivy gave a funny little scream, and stared as the blood ran down and soaked into Frosty's collar.

The Maggot gazed up at Frosty as if he was fascinated. He took a step back, holding his knife poised. 'That was the first part of the lesson, Frosty.'

Adam walked into the centre of the Barn. 'Turn round, Mr Maggs!' he said.

The Maggot did turn round, startled. He was not accustomed to interruptions. 'Who the hell are you?'

'Drop the knife on the floor.'

The Maggot allowed himself a slow smile, amused, challenging. Perhaps he thought this boy's strange anger was about to break out. What he couldn't know was that Adam's anger was different from most people's. It did not make him lose control; Adam's fury was ironclad.

'Better keep out of this, little boy,' the Maggot said softly. 'This is not for kids.'

The knife was raised towards Adam's face. 'Drop the knife,' Adam said.

'I always do the face first,' the Maggot said pleasantly. His thoughts were shaped by violence.

'I usually do it last,' Adam said.

The Maggot frowned. He'd been in many situations like this and he knew how they went. Perhaps there would be some muttered taunting, an insult or two. It was the same with movements. He had an instinctive knowledge of what people did with their fists, and how they balanced their bodyweight.

And he knew in advance, almost as if it had been rehearsed to precision, the intended pathway of knife-blade and knife-point. He anticipated its careful draughtsmanship.

But this boy was not following the script. He did none of the expected things – he just stood there. A mere boy!

Adam did what no other opponent had ever done. He brought his right hand hard up on the Maggot's wrist and clamped it there. Then – instead of trying to twist the knife free – he raised the Maggot's arm high above his head, held his own body well clear, and forced the older man backwards.

Christ! The Maggot could hardly believe it! He found himself losing his balance, staggering and back-stepping, with his arm held straight up over his head like a child in school wanting the toilet. He was forced backwards to the wall, where Adam crashed him down on to a bale of straw pushed against the wall. At this point he dropped the knife. A proper opponent would have kicked it away out of reach, but Adam ignored it. He clamped his other hand round the Maggot's throat and slammed his head back against the wall, holding him there. The Maggot was stapled to the wall by Adam's grip.

He had a moment of shock, an appreciation of danger. This had never happened before. He had allowed himself to be outnumbered. Big Ben was useless. Thatch might have been some help, but there were all these kids – *big* kids! – closing in.

'Don't try anything, mate,' he growled at Adam. His voice rasped. 'I'm older than you and a hell of a lot smarter.'

'But I'm *angrier*,' Adam said softly.

Adam was in command. But the others – Hamish, Abigail, Molly – knew there was nothing certain about this. The direction of danger could at any moment reverse itself.

The Maggot was chilled to his very heart. This boy was beyond anything he had ever experienced. He must be mad! How could the Maggot be expected to cope with a lunatic?

'How old are you?' Adam demanded.

What the hell had *that* got to do with anything? 'I'm sixty-two,' the Maggot heard himself saying.

'Then it's time you retired,' Adam said quietly.

'Oi, mate.' This was Thatch, making an effort. But he was hemmed in by two girls. *Girls?* Dimly Thatch's battered understanding sensed their strong physical presence. And there was that other boy, the one with the posh voice.

'Stay there!' Adam said. The Maggot was mesmerised,

there was no disobeying this boy. 'You wanted my drawings? Well, you shall have one – one of your very own!' Amazingly, the Maggot stayed put, rubbing his neck, as Adam walked away.

Hamish stepped quietly forward and picked up the knife, for safety.

Adam grabbed an old stool and sat himself on it, facing the Maggot. There was a pad, and some drawing things, abandoned there since earlier in the summer. He started to draw, looking up briefly at his sitter.

In the half light of the thunderstorm, Adam saw with a thin and ruthless clarity. As a younger boy he'd drawn cartoon strips; and he drew them *fast*. He'd never lost that ability. What he drew now was a cartoon portrait – done with the precise economy of controlled anger. The lines appeared on the paper with savage speed.

The Maggot continued to sit, caught in fascinated fear by the inscrutable authority of this schoolboy in front of him. This was his unmaking, and the silent watching audience set a seal on it.

And the drawing? A hangman's noose in the foreground, knotted, black and terrible, savagely scribbled with a 6B pencil. Below it the Maggot, staring up at the noose in mortal fear, so terrified that he couldn't stand. Two shadowy executioners stood with him, one on each side, holding him up. His feet were off the floor. There was no shading, no crosshatching, no time for any of that, only a sharp fierce use of line. Hints of a barred window suggested a setting, complete and terrifying, like a prophecy. The flat edge of a stick of charcoal added the final shadows.

The others, nervously, edged close to look at the drawing. At the bottom Adam scrawled *Mr Maggs' Finest Hour.*

Adam stood up so violently that the wooden stool fell backwards with a crash and everybody flinched. He thrust his sketchpad in front of the Maggot's eyes. 'A portrait of *you!*' he said. 'The *real* you! And you can keep it as a reminder.'

The Maggot took in the drawing. He rubbed his chin nervously and looked repeatedly up and down, from Adam's face to the drawing and back again.

Foolish, Hamish thought to himself. A brilliant stroke – but foolish to give it to the Maggot, who would just tear it up. So, in his best public school voice, educated to elegant perfection, he said, 'I have a better idea, old chap. *We'll* keep the drawing – and if ever you lay a finger on anyone else it will be released for sale.'

It took a minute for this to sink in. Hamish continued. 'It will be displayed in every bally art gallery. *And all your friends will know exactly who it is.*'

Adam had found the Maggot's secret terror, the hangman's rope. It was like a worm, a coiled parasite deep in his stomach. It had always been there. 'Listen!' he said. He seemed about to make a speech, some kind of announcement perhaps. But it was never uttered.

'There's a train to London in half an hour,' Abigail said firmly.

Thatch moved forward and put his huge hand on the Maggot's shoulder. 'Let's go, boss,' he said. 'There's too many of 'em.'

Slowly the Maggot rose to his feet. He moved towards the door, stunned, muttering something about crazy people, and how could he be expected to deal with lunatics? But everyone knew these were excuses to himself. Big Ben had managed to get to his feet, recovering a little now that the thunder was moving on.

The three men left the Barn and squelched away on the rain-soaked footpath.

Ivy said brightly to Adam, 'Will you do one of us? Just me and my dad?'

'No,' Adam said quietly. He went over to Frosty Winters and held out his hand. Frosty knew what he meant. He pulled out his wallet and removed a thick wad of banknotes. He didn't bother to count them, he just handed over the whole lot.

Adam counted five pound-notes from the bundle and gave them back to Frosty. 'You'll need to go somewhere,' he said. 'And a new shirt.'

Then there were just the four of them, left on their own in the Barn. Abigail took Hamish's hand and led him to the staircase. The other two followed them up – and Hamish was welcomed in.

He sat with Abigail on the bed, facing the tiny fireplace. Molly and Adam sat on a couple of old chairs.

Knee to knee, they counted the money that Frosty had given back, and found it amounted roughly to what a farm-worker earned in a year.

They should have felt excited and triumphant. And they tried to behave as if they did. But, in truth, they were depressed and tired.

And – they slowly realised – *hungry*.

'I came down here to take us all out for a fish-and-chip supper,' Hamish said. 'So what about it?'

But they didn't want to be with other people. They wanted to stay in the Barn until they began to feel more like themselves, until they'd decided what they were going to say, and who was going to be told. So Hamish offered to go into town and bring back fish-and-chips for all of them.

Adam went down to the big door with him to check that the coast was clear.

Hamish was back at the Barn half an hour later, with fish-and-chips for four, two bottles of fizzy drink to share – and the news that a second atomic bomb had been dropped on Japan.

A second B-29 had taken off. Hamish heard about it at the fish-shop. The city of Nagasaki had been annihilated and around forty thousand people incinerated in an instant.

Nagasaki! How strangely things turn out! We hardly gave them a thought, Molly recalls with shame.

A van pulls up outside the gallery and heavy brown-paper packages are being unloaded. They contain the catalogues for the Swales Exhibition.

They are expensive and smart, with over two hundred reproductions of Adam's work, flawlessly printed. Molly herself is in twenty-eight of them. People will be sick of the sight of me, she thinks to herself.

She observes that the catalogues were printed in Japan, in Nagasaki.

Molly believes that everything that happened in 1945 is safely folded up and tucked away. But it isn't.

She remembers with a sudden clarity how the last of the storm cloud cleared and the sun came out, dazzling in the western sky. It flooded the little room with an astonishing warm radiance, like a new dawn rising in the west.

50

They told no one what had happened.

And they never saw Frosty again. Two days later Ivy left as well.

She said no goodbyes. On the kitchen table, she left a note for Auntie Betty. It thanked her for letting her stay and explained that she was going to Carlisle to live with her husband's family. '*Abigail will explain about him,*' Ivy had written.

Years later, at a family funeral, Abigail saw Ivy again. Her husband had come back from the Far East early in 1946 and set himself up as a car mechanic. They had seven children. 'Right little tykes, all of them,' Ivy said happily.

But still there was no Japanese surrender. The world waited.

A woman came to Great Deeping to give a talk in the town hall about conditions in post-war Europe. Abigail persuaded Molly to go with her.

The woman was a photographer working for the United Nations Relief and Rehabilitation scheme. She had followed the British army as it had advanced through Germany. She showed films she had made herself with a cine-camera. There was no sound, but the woman gave her own running commentary.

The small audience – around twenty-five people – saw bleak pictures of women (thousands of them) queuing for food, each with a single bag or bucket, amid an endless landscape of rubble; they saw people lined up in rows, looking scared. There were bewildered children whose families had vanished; a child searching inside the pockets of a corpse; a British captain in despair because he'd hardly enough food for his men and now he had a thousand surrendered SS troops to feed as well.

It was hopeless, a never-ending tragedy of desolation. Long processions of despairing faces, gazing dumbly at the camera. In Germany, Austria, Poland, Czechoslovakia. Yet, in spite of everything, there were helpers, groups of volunteers organised by churches, and individual people.

Afterwards Abigail stayed behind to talk to the presenter.

Two days later she told her mum she wasn't going back to school next term. Mrs Murfitt raised all the obvious objections – but half-heartedly, as if she'd understood Abigail before Abigail understood herself.

'You not old enough,' she said wearily.

'I can leave school at fifteen.'

'When you started at the High School, I signed

an agreement that you'd stay until you were sixteen.'

'Well, I *will* be sixteen in October! What's the point of going back just for two or three weeks?'

'Abigail, what is it you want to do?'

'I want to work for the UN Relief.'

There was a silence as Mrs Murfitt realised that it all made sense. Perhaps she saw the rest of her life ahead of her, alone most of the time. 'Yes,' she said at last. 'Of course. But you're far too young. They won't let you . . .'

'I know that,' Abigail said. 'But they also need people at their office in London. I'll be some kind of assistant, even a cleaner! I'm not too young for that. Or I'll learn to be a typist. Then when I'm a year or two older, they'll send me out to do a proper job.'

'You used to want to be an engine driver,' Mrs Murfitt said sadly. She remembered the three-year-old Abigail, the five-year-old, the ten-year-old. She remembered all the Abigails.

'I know, and I still think it's the best job in the world. But how many women train drivers have you seen?'

Mrs Murfitt nodded. There wouldn't be many women operating crossing-gates either, she thought, once the men were all demobbed.

'Mum, I want to be useful.'

Molly was amazed when she heard about this. In her house, such a decision would take months to settle, but Abigail had arranged it in ten minutes! In her turn, Abigail was surprised to find that the greatest resistance came from Molly. 'I can't remember *anything* without you in it!' Molly said piteously. 'Nothing will be the same if you go away!'

'But you'll leave too,' Abigail said. 'You'll go to university and do your archaeology!'

'But not *yet!*' Molly said in anguish.

Molly thought she could never forgive Abigail. Who would she talk to at school, on the bus? 'We're joined at the hip,' she said.

'You have Adam,' Abigail pointed out.

'That's not the same thing!' Molly snapped. There were a thousand daily matters where a boy was no use at all. Even Adam. *Especially* Adam.

But Molly felt a little hidden tremor of excitement. Everything was changing. Fastenings were coming loose.

The money that Frosty had handed over was problematic. Did it belong to Adam, or should it be paid back to Paterson Royce, who had used his own money to buy back some of the drawings?

Adam cycled over to Soham to consult Mr Fraser.

It was a strange day. The air was warm like midsummer, the sky as low and colourless as winter. Nothing was clear. Was he still an artist, or was he someone who'd stopped being an artist? Had he stopped for ever?

At the Frasers' studio, no art was done that day.

Adam helped the old man to strip and clean an old platen printing press.

Marion Fraser came into the workshop and told them that the Prime Minister was going to broadcast to the nation that night. 'I've just heard it on the wireless,' she said. 'The Japs have probably surrendered. At last!'

How strange it seemed! Everything was changing, from a world at war to a world at peace. Yet there was no thunderclap, the clouds didn't clear, the birds failed to burst into song – nothing stirred at all.

Mr Fraser went back to his printing press and Adam helped Mrs Fraser to make sandwiches. He was aware of her blue shirt, her bare arms, her throat and neck, her closeness. She buttered bread and sliced tomatoes in the same way that she sketched landscapes, unhurriedly, with that impenetrable grace.

'When I was fourteen,' she said, 'I decided I didn't want to be an artist. I never wanted to draw or paint again. So I lit a bonfire in my father's garden and I burnt everything. My sketchbooks, pencils, pastels. Everything.'

The hairs on her arm brushed his.

'Then I started having nightmares. I dreamt that all my teeth came loose and my eyeballs fell out of their sockets. I awoke with a terrible pain from the top of my head to my jawbone. That happened every night. After about a week I bought a new sketchbook and started again.'

'The nightmares stopped?'

'Yes.'

They sat outside. As the three of them reached for sandwiches, for the jam, or for biscuits, hands touched briefly, a shoulder was pressed, their feet got in the way of each other. They talked in low voices. Adam loved being with these two.

Afterwards, Mr and Mrs Fraser went indoors and Adam sat for a while outside. A few early raindrops fell, threatening a downpour. Through the open door he saw the two of them inside, standing, silently holding each other. He felt an overwhelming desire to be with Molly.

51

Japan had surrendered at last. The Prime Minister, Mr Attlee, confirmed the news in a radio broadcast. 'The last of our enemies is laid low,' he said. He ordered two days of holiday to celebrate this final victory.

The people of Great Deeping celebrated all through the night. The eating started at around eight – but this time they meant business. VE-Day had meant peace in Europe, this was the *total end* of World War Two, the first day of peace across the world.

Children stayed up long after bedtime, unable to believe their luck. At around midnight everyone followed the brass band in a torchlight procession through the streets. Then they brought out gramophones and played their favourite records, danced until their feet were sore and their legs ached, and then there was spontaneous community singing.

It went on for hours, until people saw in amazement that the sky was paling. They'd been up all night! As the sun rose they talked quietly, finding new things to say to neighbours they talked to every day. Teapots were filled, toast was made, eggs were boiled – all brought into the bright morning-lit streets.

By early afternoon, everyone was exhausted.

The shops were shut and there were abandoned tables and chairs in the streets. Front doors were left open so that you could see through shadowy passages to sleepy back gardens. Bicycles sprawled in unfamiliar places. A wary dog hunted for titbits under the tables, keeping an eye out for cats doing the same. A solitary woman gathered up her crockery, helped by her granddaughter, clutching spoons.

The town had a sleep-spell on it. In the streets, there were no children. Many of the youngest had fallen asleep wherever they happened to be when the need came on them – in the wrong houses, curled up in strange armchairs, unfamiliar grown-ups keeping a sleepy eye on them.

Around midday, Molly and Adam slipped away to the mere, unnoticed. Abigail had gone off somewhere with Hamish. Everyone in the town seemed to have found a place to sleep.

Through the long afternoon the two of them swam and swam again, towelled themselves dry and towelled themselves again. Between times, they lay in the warm sun and ate plums, biscuits and crushed slices of cake. Their bodies glowed.

Molly sat with a towel across her knees, the portable typewriter on her lap. By mid-afternoon she had almost finished the clean typewritten copy of her report.

A MEDIAEVAL JETTY AT DEEPING MERE
by
Molly Barnes
August 1945.

She was a slow one-finger typist, but methodical and accurate – you had to be, because mistakes could not be corrected. You just had to put in a fresh sheet of paper and type the page again.

'You promised,' she said – and Adam knew what she meant. Weeks ago, they'd tried taking photographs of the jetty to be included in the report, but they had only a cheap camera and the results were poor. So Adam had promised he would make some sketches.

But that was before his drawings had been stolen.

Molly completed her final sentence, and said again, 'You *promised.*'

They swam again. Afterwards, Molly lay down with a handkerchief over her eyes, sun-dazed and sleepy. Adam sat beside her, watching the rise and fall of her breathing. He could see her chest leaping minutely, almost imperceptibly, with her heartbeat.

The eye inside his head went roving. His longings and his skills assembled themselves into a purpose. He picked up a pencil and started. Molly appeared to the right of centre page, standing, seen from behind, but still recognisably Molly, tall, wearing a long flowing dress (where had *that* come from?). She was standing at the edge of a small lake. Recovering its old confidence, his pencil shaded in the water. There were dark rocks, and tall cliffs on the other side of the lake. It was like an old wood-engraving, a twilight dream.

But what was this long-gowned Molly looking at? On the other side of the lake he had left undrawn a white space in the shadow of the mountains.

He became aware that she had woken up and was kneeling beside him. 'Guinevere,' she said. 'Looking for Lancelot.' Adam didn't know whether it was Guinevere or the Queen of Sheba. She might have been Princess Elizabeth or Vera Lynn for all he cared. It didn't need words.

But no Lancelot appeared on the far side of the water. The eye inside Adam's head saw differently, wilfully, and what it saw appeared on the page almost before it appeared in his head.

A fox.

Just a fox. Almost part of the darkness, and too far to be seen in detail, but clearly a fox. Hungry-looking, wily, on edge. Its ears were alert, its eyes sharp, and a curling white line along its snout and jaw was good-humouredly greedy.

Molly's body goose-pimpled all over and she felt the hairs on her arms stand on end. The real Molly looked at Molly-in-the-picture, and Molly-in-the-picture watched the fox.

'It's just a sketch,' he said mildly. 'I'll work it up properly, with pastels and chalk.' Then he added, 'I did these as well. While you were asleep.'

He pulled out some drawings of the jetty – a few false starts, then two complete and perfect illustrations. One was a close-up to show the precise alignment of the stones, the other showed the jetty in its setting, sloping down into the water of the mere. Beyond were the ever-stretching Fens, and in the far distance the tiny double-stump of Ely Cathedral on the heat-hazed line of the horizon – two mediaeval stone buildings, one humble, the other magnificent.

Molly put her title-page back into the typewriter and added: with illustrations by Adam Swales.

'Let's swim,' Adam said.

Hand in hand they walked into the shallows, squeezing the soft gritty mud between their toes. Then in unison, with an end-of-the-day unhurriedness, they struck out and swam to the middle of the mere.

When they came out they were rosy in the light of the warm setting sun. They dressed, packed up their things, and walked back towards Paradise Barn, through the seeding dusty cow-parsley.

'Why didn't you marry him?'

Molly and the interviewer are sitting upstairs, quietly drinking tea, with Molly's granddaughter. There are no cameras or microphones, no one listening.

'I didn't think it would work.'

'But you lived with him?'

'Yes. On and off. More on than off.' Molly notices

Carrie listening, all ears, and watchful.

It was a habit of his to go away on an impulse. He couldn't help himself. Mostly, he came back – but there had been one or two occasions when she'd gone in search of him. Once she found him among the summer millionaires in Saint-Tropez. Another time, in the middle of an arctic winter on the bitter northern-most tip of Norway.

Through some hidden dynamic, some of his most famous paintings coincided with these trips. A thought flashed through her mind and was gone before she could grasp it. *The fox comes out in search of what it needs, then slips away.*

Molly accepted the disappearances calmly. After all, she reminded herself, they would have never met at all if he hadn't left his school friends and made off into the unknown on the day he was evacuated.

This time, however, they were both into their late seventies. *Should* she be worried?

'You and he have a daughter, I believe?'

'Yes. Anna – she went to work in Africa.'

'And she married?'

'Yes. She married a South African lawyer. They both work in Cambridge now.'

'And this is their daughter?'

The interviewer has hardly been able to take her eyes off the child. Carrie's skin is the colour of milk chocolate, and her eyes – that great rarity – are blue.

'Have you enjoyed your grandfather's exhibition?'

She nods. 'I'm going to be an artist,' she says.

They are back in the gallery when one of the attendants hurries in. 'There's a package,' he says. 'For Professor Barnes.' He peers closely at labels and stamps. 'I think it's from . . . *Peru*?'

Molly's heart sinks. What use is a package?

So it's her granddaughter who tears open the wrapping and spreads the contents on the table. There are sheets of art paper, each with a drawing – some in pencil, others in charcoal and pastels, pen-and-ink.

Most are portraits of Molly, thirty-four of them. Tender, breathtakingly lovely. As a girl, as a young woman, as an older woman. Seven are nudes.

Molly's grip on reality is in danger of slipping.

'Who's this?' Carrie asks.

It is a drawing of a girl aged about ten or eleven, wearing running clothes. Molly steadies herself. 'That's your mother,' she says.

'And this one?'

There is a small child, a baby just at the moment of turning into a toddler. She is plump, with a sagging nappy, gripping a chair-leg with one hand, and about to take a step away.

'That's you.'

People are pressing forward to see the drawings laid out on the table. 'It's like getting a love letter,' someone says.

Molly shakes her head. 'No. Love letters are about the future.'

'There must be thousands of pounds' worth of art in that package,' someone remarks.

But Molly feels unutterably cast down. What use is a bundle of pictures?

In the main gallery, a tall white-haired man is chatting to the Curator. He is casually dressed, some country person, she thinks.

'That overhead light – it's draining the life out of that painting! It will have to be moved. You do see that?'

The Curator is dismayed. She has just realised who he is.

'But I *can't* move it!' she cries. 'They've all been numbered and labelled and hung in their places. And I can't have the catalogues reprinted – they cost *thousands*!' She is having a professional panic. Disgrace confronts her. 'There isn't *time*! And there are the audio-guides too!'

'There's a space in the West Gallery,' Adam says. 'It will be perfect there. All you need to do is mount a small notice here explaining where the picture has been moved to. It *can* be done.'

Nothing so dreadful has ever happened to the Curator. She hurries off blindly, not knowing how to deal with this.

Adam sees a pad of gallery notepaper. He sits at a table, and when the Curator returns she sees he has divided the page into four pencilled frames. In the first, a huge black-browed Adam Swales glares furiously down at a tiny Curator, looking up at him like a guilty schoolgirl. In the second, they are reversed. Anger flashes from her eyes as she glares down at an ugly little boy with a shifty look. In the third frame, two of the staff are carrying away a painting.

The Curator is astonished at the speed with which he has worked. She watches as he draws the final picture: the two of them embracing. Only her face can be seen, in profile – dark eyes half-closed, her face intelligent and lovely, an *Arabian Nights* princess with 21st-century style.

He turns over the drawing and writes on the back: *for Alice Shankar, in gratitude for a wonderful exhibition.* He signs it off with his monogram, a capital S superimposed on an A.

He knows my name! she thinks to herself.

'That's for you,' he says. 'Now we must make it true.' She's given no choice. He takes her in his arms and hugs her ('He's a polar bear!' she tells her family later).

'Is Professor Barnes somewhere in that crowd in the other gallery?' he asks.

'Yes,' Dr Shankar says breathlessly. 'They're just finishing the filming.'

'Have we nearly done?' Carrie asks.

The interviewer explains. 'We just have to do the intro.'

A make-up artist does something to Molly's face.

Screens, lights and cameras are shifted around, quietly and without fuss.

'I'll begin by speaking to camera,' the Interviewer explains, 'then I'll ask you when you first met Adam. You answer the question – and that's all.'

There is a stirring near the entrance. Molly sees a white head. Someone tall has come quietly in at the back.

Their eyes meet across the crowded room. She is restrained, no one sees her joy. His head disappears as he bends down to his granddaughter. She can see them with her mind's eye, beaming at each other.

The filming starts. The interviewer reads from her cue.

'Molly Barnes is Professor of Archaeology at Cambridge, Fellow of St Adelaide's College, and honoured all over the world for her work. She has written and edited numerous books, she has five honorary doctorates and is currently Adviser to Her Majesty the Queen on archaeological sites on Crown property. Professor Barnes has led digs in Cambodia, Thailand, Brazil and China. In recent years, however, she has returned to her first love – the archaeology of mediaeval and Anglo-Saxon England.

'But there is a side to her life that is not connected with archaeology. For over sixty years she has been a close friend and partner to the artist Adam Swales, who is the subject of tonight's special extended edition of the Art Today *programme.'*

The Interviewer turns to Molly. *'Professor Barnes, when did you first meet Adam Swales?'*

'In 1940,' Molly says. 'We were ten years old. When the first wave of the blitz hit London, thousands of children were evacuated to the country. Adam was one of them. He came to our house – and stayed there.'

'Cut,' someone says quietly. 'Thank you, Professor,' the Interviewer says. 'That's perfect.'

It's over, finished at last. They can go home. In the street outside the gallery, Adam turns his attention to his granddaughter. There is a deedy look in his eye. He puts his fingers under her chin and tilts her head up towards him. 'Granny said in one of her letters that you want to be an artist.'

'Yes.'

He takes her right hand and inspects her nails and fingertips. They are spotless. 'Have you got a sketchbook?'

She faces him squarely, eyes raised, challenging. 'No,' she says. She does not flinch.

She is wearing a mauve shoulder-bag. Her grandfather reaches down and unzips it. Out come three books – by Arthur Ransome, Philippa Pearce, and Malorie Blackman. Then a black hard-covered notebook, held shut with elastic. 'What's this?'

In the late afternoon sunlight the crowds of people hurrying along Oxford Street skirt around this small drama, unaware.

'It's *private*!' Carrie says fiercely. 'You *mustn't*

read it!' He holds the notebook high, out of her reach.

He doesn't read it. But he flips through the pages with his thumb, enough to see that the notebook is filled with tiny writing.

'Writers are as good as artists,' he says to her. '*Almost.*'

She grabs back her notebook and concentrates on putting everything tidily in her bag. 'Anyway, you said you wouldn't come back for the exhibition,' she says, accusing.

'Exhibitions can look after themselves,' Adam says. 'That's not why I came back.'

She absorbs this, understands, and approves. Then she says, pleading, 'Can we go home now?'

Molly absorbs it too. She is suddenly joyous, light-hearted.

'Back to Great Deeping,' Adam says.

They could get a taxi. But old habits die hard, and they set off in search of a bus to King's Cross. Hand in hand with their granddaughter, laughing about something, soon they are lost in the crowds.

In writing this story, I consulted many sources, one of which proved especially helpful. This was *The London Blitz: a Fireman's Tale* by Cyril Demarne, published in 1980. The episode involving German prisoners-of-war shouting *Sieg Heil!* is based on a true incident described in this book.

The V-1 flying bombs (also known as doodle-bugs or buzzbombs) stopped arriving over London in January 1945 as advancing allied troops on the continent captured and destroyed the launch sites. But they resumed for a while in March. One of the last V-2s fell in Tottenham Court Road, London, on 25th March.

The United Nations Relief and Rehabilitation organisation which Abigail planned to join was not – despite its name – connected with the United Nations of today. It was established in 1943 to provide help for the millions of people displaced by the War. The United Nations as we now know it was not founded until 1945.

The tanner that Mrs Ogmore refers to was a small silver sixpenny coin, the equivalent in today's money is only 2.5p.

For more adventures featuring Molly,
Abigail and Adam . . .

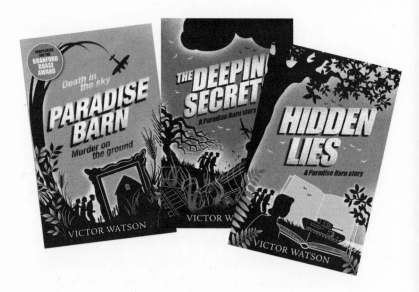